DOGMEAT SAMOSA

Stanley Gazemba

Regal House Publishing

Published by
Regal House Publishing, LLC
Raleigh, NC 27612
All rights reserved

ISBN -13 (paperback): 9781947548558
ISBN -13 (epub): 9781947548565
ISBN -13 (mobi): 9781947548817
Library of Congress Control Number: 2019931632

Most of the stories in this collection were made possible by a grant from the Miles Morland Foundation.

Interior and cover design by Lafayette & Greene
lafayetteandgreene.com
Cover images © by C.B. Royal
Author photograph by Drix Photography

Regal House Publishing, LLC
https://regalhousepublishing.com

Printed in the United States of America

To the memories of Susan Linnée,
my mentor and long-time editor, and Patrick Adika,
my kid bro who fixed both our computer problems.
Strange that you bowed off the stage in the same way.

CONTENTS

PEMA PEPONI

Mukabwa, sitting atop the cracked cement stairs and leisurely smoking a cigarette, was sick of the pestering village women. He glared at them through reddened eyes, tempted to kick them out of his office and to tell them never to come back. There were four who he found particularly irritating; thin bird-like peasant women, toughened in the open sun of the farms, were fronting the bargaining, and had the pointed stares of street mongrels eyeing rock-wielding kids. They kept moving to and from the spot in the parking lot where the rest of the group were bunched, waiting resignedly. He gave them all an acid stare as they came back to crowd at the foot of the stairs, blocking other business that might have been more lucrative.

Mukabwa took a long puff of his cigarette and blew the smoke out slowly so it formed a long column-like jet. Then, feeling his nerves begin to fray, he spat angrily in the shriveled flowers at the foot of the stairs. He needed a drink.

One of the women, named Hannah, started walking in Mukabwa's direction, adjusting the knot in her tightly wound cloth belt. The rest stood wailing demonstratively, flinging their arms up above their heads and beating their chests as tears streamed down their cheeks.

The women clustered around the beat-up Datsun. The pick-up leaned precariously on its hind wheels, the metal railings poking through the patched-up tarpaulin like the ribs

1

of a starving mongrel. The vehicle was swathed in broken branches and red ribbons, a grim indication of the job for which it had been hired.

The men stood in a somber bunch a little distance from the truck, having resigned themselves to the long wait when it became apparent their attempts at bargaining were fruitless. Leaning against the twisted trunk of a guava tree, the driver finished his cigarette and lit another from the stub. He was in a sour mood and had argued bitterly with the party about the time they were taking to settle the matter. It was a long drive to the village where the burial would be held, and dark clouds gathered ominously overhead. The last thing he needed was to get stuck in the rut-marked cattle-track of a road leading from the village after a downpour.

Hannah approached Mukabwa, her wide nostrils flared with emotion, her tear-filled eyes fixed beseechingly on his face, a bright nylon scarf wound tightly around her head, pulling the skin tautly across pronounced bones and sunken cheeks.

"Mukabwa, listen to me. I plead with you," she cried piteously, her gaze fixed on him. "I am an old woman, and I am begging you. Give us our John so that we can get on our way before the rain starts. Please soften your heart, Mukabwa, and listen to us. Remember you are also of the clan, and that your day will come too."

"Listen, woman," said Mukabwa gruffly, shaking off her clinging hand. "I have told you what needs to be done. I won't repeat myself. And don't you imagine that you can make me change my mind with your useless tears."

"But you surely can't be—"

"You can save your words for another occasion, woman. I am not here to bandy words with anyone. Either you do as I say or you get out of here. You are blocking the way for other customers, you know. Or do you imagine that you are the only ones I have to attend to?"

"My son, Mukabwa," pleaded the distraught woman. "Mind the words you say to people who are in mourning. Remember I am the age of your mother, and that I—"

"Ha! Are you now threatening me with a curse, woman?" asked Mukabwa with a snide laugh. "Is that what you are saying? Well, you can try it on someone else," he said rising. "This one here is way beyond such old-woman nonsense. Now I think I'll go off for a drink. You people are making my head spin with your empty words that go round and round like a cobweb. As if a man can live on words. Or is it that you want me to give you the body as it is? Is that what you want, woman? If that is the case, then go right ahead and collect it!" He gestured irritably at the open door. "The door is wide open, as you can see. Go right in!"

"I am begging you, Mukabwa," said the woman, gazing at him reverently.

"Now, get out of my office," he ordered, shaking a thick finger in the woman's face. "Go on and join your other clanspeople over there!" With that he swung the door closed, descended the stairs, and strode down the narrow path that snaked through the overgrown hospital grounds toward the kiosk. He didn't bother to lock the door. His was perhaps the only office in the world that one could leave unattended and go away on a long vacation without fear of vandalism.

Mukabwa whistled softly to himself as he went, his feet

squelching in the muck that had spilled inside his oversize, standard-issue white Wellingtons. As he neared the kiosk he dipped his hands into his roomy pockets to take stock of his takings for the morning. The mostly low-denomination notes were grubby and crumpled in the manner of illegal earnings hastily stuffed away; the coins, grime-coated and nicked, like loose change that even a beggar might disdain. As soiled as the money might be, there was a marvelous sense of power in having a full pocket; and as aggravating as his customers might be, he wouldn't be quitting his job any time soon, Mukabwa determined. The hospital cashier might as well use the miserly salary he doled out at the end of the month to buy himself lunch, for all he cared.

"You are early today, Mukabwa," said Rhoda, the kiosk owner. She was a short thick-set woman whose shiny eyes were constantly shifting. Rhoda knew all the subordinate staff of the hospital because almost all of them maintained accounts with her, whether for vegetables, sugar, or other groceries that they paid for at the end of the month. All the men, too, held accounts for the moonshine Rhoda sold under the counter, which provided her main source of income. Her customers had to place their orders through a tiny hole cut into the rusty mesh wire in the shop window, which protected her wares from petty shoplifters and the prying eyes of any unfamiliar hospital official who might chance to pass by. Rhoda passed a plastic bottle through the hole before Mukabwa had the opportunity to order his usual. "Business must be good today."

Mukabwa grunted in reply and settled down on the bench by the kiosk, stretching his legs out before him. He rammed the base of the bottle twice against the heel of his hand, watching keenly as the bubbles rose from the base to the top of the clear liquid. It was a practice he had picked up in the town shebeens,[1] one intended to verify the potency of the contents. Satisfied he hadn't been cheated, Mukabwa snapped the seal with his thumb, twisted the plastic cap, and took a long leisurely swig, his protruding Adam's apple jerking up and down as he swallowed.

"Aaaah!" he sighed, rubbing the back of his hand over his wet lips.

"How does it feel today?" Rhoda always asked him that, as if she had given him a slow-acting poison and was eager to know if it was taking effect. Mukabwa nodded and raised the bottle to his lips again. He was not in the mood for small talk this morning.

"Someone must have given you a rough time," she remarked at length, arranging bunches of *sukuma-wiki*[2] and pyramids of cherry-red tomatoes on her tray beside the counter.

Mukabwa nodded and tossed back the last of his drink. Grimacing, he held up the empty bottle and eyed it malevolently before tossing it on the trash pile next to the kiosk. He snapped his finger and Rhoda handed him another bottle through the hole, which he similarly inspected and opened.

When Mukabwa rose to leave a short while later, the whites of his eyes had reddened. His steps were a little unsteady as

---

[1] Off-license bars in the slum districts of a town, often composed of wooden or metal shacks, where cheap and illicit liquor is sold, not to mention cheap sex!

[2] A common name for kale or collard greens, a staple in many poor Kenyan households.

he cut across the weedy field back to his office, the tails of his worn overcoat flapping against his wet Wellingtons.

Halfway across the field Mukabwa paused to regard the expansive hospital and the doctors within, busy applying their book knowledge to treat the various ailments of their patients. After six years of hospital employment, he well understood the process. Usually patients arrived at the main entrance, where their details were taken before they were ushered in to see the doctor. If they were lucky, the sick would be sent to the pharmacy for drugs before being discharged; otherwise, patients were sent to the wards where their ordeal would begin. More often than not, their trials would encompass a fateful trip to the X-ray room at the farthest end of the hallway. And too bad for them if the doctor determined that a trip to surgery was in store, the dreaded room where shiny sterilized blades would be put to work.

But it was the unfortunate lot who failed to survive this complex chain who were of particular interest to Mukabwa. Their journey would finally end at his little office. After all their knowledge had failed them, the doctors, with an air of washing their hands of dust and grime, delivered the patient to a village fellow who had hardly mastered elementary school. Now *that* was something to think about, Mukabwa mused. Despite the important role he played in hospital affairs, his office was cramped and muggy, set aside from the spacious rest in a corner overgrown with weeds and crumbling with neglect. And yet it was him, Mukabwa, who drove the last nail into the casket, who was the final caretaker for the patients in this convoluted process of pain and medication.

Hannah, together with three other women, waited for him by the chipped cement stairs. She tugged at his arm with her spidery fingers as he climbed the stairs. "You really are not going to change your mind about this, are you, Mukabwa?"

Mukabwa paused, his hand on the steel handle of his office door, before slowly turning and leveling his gaze on the women who clustered behind him like a flock of frightened hens. As one, the women retreated, surprised at the coldness in the depths of his now bloodshot eyes.

"Go away," he said simply, but with a sinking finality. "I told you I do not eat grass. Do not make me repeat myself. I need money."

Without another word, Mukabwa strode into his office, collected the full slop bucket he had left in the corridor, and threw the noxious smelling contents down the length of the room toward the women, who shrieked and sprang backward.

When the women returned to the pickup truck, crestfallen and empty-handed, the driver gave the spokesman of the little party a piece of his mind, gesticulating angrily at the thick grey cloud slouching steadily across the sky from the distant line of hills. Thereafter, the driver climbed into the cab and, with vehement finality, slammed the door shut.

There was only one choice left to the mourning women. One of the group unwound her headscarf and spread it out upon the ground. She reached into the neckline of her white dress and drew out the little money-pouch that rested next to her breast at the end of a string. From within the pouch, she withdrew a few coins, counting them carefully against the sunlight before tossing them on the scarf. The others similarly gathered around the scarf, each reaching for their own money pouches.

The hospital had suffered a simultaneous cut to both power and water supplies that morning and Mr. Karani, the administrator, was more than ready for his lunch hour. He had had to spend hours on the phone pleading with the power and water companies to reinstate their services, to give him a little more time to settle the hospital's massive debts. And the circulating rumors of an impending strike by the hospital staff—who were owed three months of salary payments—had not made his morning any easier. These upheavals, he knew, were instigated by the much-publicized inspection visit this coming Friday by a high-powered team from the Ministry headquarters.

As Mr. Karani circled the back of the administration block toward the staff parking, he saw the little party clustered in the yard outside the morgue. He watched as one of the women gathered the edges of the scarf into a bundle and made her way toward the little stone building at the edge of the compound, the others following behind.

Mukabwa counted the money a second time and then tucked it away inside his pocket. He grinned at the women, revealing massive brown teeth. "I'll have him ready in five minutes' time," he assured the women, even as he ushered them all out and locked the door behind them.

Unbeknownst to Mukabwa, the hospital administrator had intercepted the women as they left the morgue. He

8

spoke briefly with them before summoning one of the men to fetch the hospital guards.

Mukabwa, meanwhile, was turning his customer over on the wet stone slab, preparing to hose him down. "And you will be needing this bath badly, you fat oaf," he remarked to the body on the table. "It's going to be a real long while down there with the maggots and ants."

It was always a source of amusement for Mukabwa that he was the last one for whom these men and women stripped—coming, as he did, after their mother, their circumciser, their doctor, their spouses, and their mistresses. And the beauty with it was that there were absolutely no qualms by the time they reached his office, be it with the minnows of the fields, or the very President of the land.

It had been quite a struggle dragging this particularly well-fed client off the trolley and onto the slab; he was short but rotund, a midget who must have worked his way through quite a number of granaries in his lifetime—*Oh, won't the grubs have a feast here!* Mukabwa thought with some delight. As he adjusted his rubber gloves and reached for the hand-held shower, Mukabwa heard a strident banging on the door.

"I said, you give me *five minutes*, didn't you people hear me?" Mukabwa hollered furiously, preparing himself to give these impertinent women another sharp tongue lashing. The one thing he could never tolerate was someone interrupting his private moment with his clients after he had collected his bribe. But as he turned toward the door he froze still. Through the opaque glass window inset in his door he could clearly make out the figures of the hospital administrator and the beefy guards, the villagers crowded behind them. In an instant, he knew precisely why they were there.

"Open up inside there!" ordered Mukabwa's boss, rattling the heavy door on its hinges.

Mukabwa knew that the administrator could not see within the room, which accorded the mortician just the slightest of opportunities—he needed to find somewhere to hide the money, and quick. When the guards shoved against that old door with their shoulders, it would come crashing in before long.

"Hey, I'm coming...give me a minute!" cried Mukabwa, his mind racing frantically, like a mouse cornered by a cat. The door rattled in its unsteady frame and the calls continued to sound from the hallway, instilling in Mukabwa a growing panic. Suddenly, a brilliant idea occurred to him. At the work table, where the corpse was stripped for his last bath, he found just the hiding spot he was looking for. *Mahali pema peponi.*[3] A nice cozy place that even the flies couldn't find.

Just after Mukabwa had emptied his pockets, the door crashed inward, the guards stumbling into room behind it. Mukabwa turned, as if surprised, his hands raised in the manner of one who had just been interrupted in a task that required the utmost concentration.

"What...?" Mukabwa began, a puzzled expression on his face. The guards, ignoring his apparent confusion—and despite the after-work drinks they had frequently shared with the mortician in the town shebeens— seized Mukabwa by the arms and pinned him to the wall.

"What's going on?" Mukabwa demanded.

---

[3] Swahili for: "A safe resting place in the after-life." A reference to heaven.

"You know what's going on," the hospital administrator stated in the calm, measured tones he reserved for agitated staff. "I've heard a lot of complaints about you, Mukabwa." The administrator gazed steadily into Mukabwa's bloodshot eyes. "Thought you were too smart, eh? Well, your forty days are here. Where's the money these people just gave you?"

"What money, sir? I do not know what you are talking about."

"Don't give me that act, Mukabwa. You either produce the money or we get it from you. Now, which do you prefer?"

From the wet table the still customer, who was at the center of all the drama, gazed unblinkingly at the ceiling. He was a sufficiently frightening sight for those not accustomed to death, with his bloated belly and puffed-up cheeks. The guards were nervous, Mukabwa could see, shifting uneasily in their boots and looking anywhere but at the cold body that lay immobile on the table. The villagers crowded, horrified, in the doorway.

"One last time—where is the money, Mukabwa?" demanded the administrator, increasingly agitated.

"I don't know what you are talking about, sir," replied Mukabwa coolly.

"The strip-search it is, I suppose," he said with a curt nod to the guards.

The guards conducted a thorough search; every item of Mukabwa's clothing was peeled away and given a shake, right down to his dirty Wellingtons. But despite their efforts, including forcing him to squat, not a shilling was found on Mukabwa's body.

"Very smart, eh?" said the administrator, his eyes glinting.

"Well, we'll shake the entire place down if we have to. And don't you imagine you'll scare us!"

Calling for a pair of latex gloves, the administrator proceeded to draw out all the trays upon which Mukabwa's charges slept in hallowed silence, with only the tiny toe tags identifying them. After an hour of fruitless searching, not a cent was found. Not even at the bottom of the slop bucket.

"Sir, what is all this about?" Mukabwa asked persistently, his wide-eyed gaze following his irate boss around, as if Mukabwa were trying in vain to convince himself that the fellow had not entirely lost his mind.

"Where is the money those people gave you?" the administrator demanded, finally losing his patience. "Where is it, Mukabwa?" His voice rose to an unsteady pitch, and a film of moisture shone across his cheeks.

"What money, sir?" Mukabwa shrugged helplessly.

The administrator had no choice but to storm out of the morgue in a defeated huff, the mystified guards following close behind. "I'll catch you, Mukabwa," he muttered to himself as he left. "I'll catch you, you foxy bastard. Some day."

The morgue attendant, meanwhile, picked up his pants and slowly started getting dressed. With the door securely locked, Mukabwa returned to his quiet client lying on the table.

"They have no manners now, do they?" he said softly, almost apologetically, to the corpse. "Storming in here to desecrate our peace. A whole bunch of idiots they are."

Replacing his rubber gloves, Mukabwa circled the body, whistling softly to himself, until he came to the head of the table.

"Now hand it back, you fat old fellow. We don't want you taking it with you to that place yonder. I suspect they don't accept our currency there. Nonetheless I must give it to you; you acted pretty coolly back there. A good customer you are. And for that you know what I'll reward you with? I'll give you a perfumed bath so that you smell like flowers for the angels when you get to the pearly gates!"

And with a hearty laugh at his own joke, Mukabwa pried open his customer's mouth and started extracting his money.

SMALL CHANGE

Godo paced the grassy yard at the front of his house, his arms swinging restlessly. He had tried sitting in his favourite spot under the fig tree at the end of the compound listening to the salaams[4] on his little transistor radio as the sun went down, but even that had been unappealing. He had fed and put to bed his youngest child, and awaited his eldest daughter to return from fetching water at the stream with her little brother so that they could prepare the evening meal.

It was unusual for Godo to be home at this hour. Usually he remained at his shop at the edge of the market square until after dark, fixing old bicycles that had broken down. Sometimes after work, if the day had been busy and his customers generous, he would pass by the village brewer's for a drink on his way home. When the brew was sweet and his pocket was full, he would give the parcel of meat he had bought at the market to one of the village lads to bring over, and Godo would stagger home sometime past midnight.

Bicycle repair was not a very lucrative job, but somehow it scraped in enough to feed the family. And Godo had been in the trade long enough to learn all the tricks. He always managed to find a new fault with someone's bicycle—a defective brake-lining, worn ball-bearings, a slow puncture, a dented rim that needed straightening, or a grease-job. If despite his best efforts he could find nothing in need of repair, he

---

[4] Swahili for 'greetings'

14

would seduce them with a gleaming side-mirror, thick saddle-padding or a custom-made mudguard with a fancy label like MLACHAKE or ROAD-RUNNER hand-painted on it. These he would attach at a little extra cost.

Tuesday, not being a market day, there had been little business at his shed, and little business for the *boda-boda*[5] operators, who lounged, bored, in the hot sun all afternoon. On market days, at least, there were basket-loads of goods and produce that needed transport home, but on Tuesdays there was nothing but the occasional customer traveling to Kilingili, whom the *boda-boda* operators would fight over loudly with traded insults and dusty scuffles. And Godo's work was inextricably tied up with the *boda-boda* operators—if they sat idle, nothing was transported, and there were fewer opportunities for bicycle repair or money for bicycle accessories. It had been a bad day for all of them.

This lack of business did little to ease Godo's worries. His eldest daughter, Adema, was preparing to join Form One at a new district boarding school a day's journey from the village. Godo had managed to save half of the required tuition, and had only a week to raise the rest—which did not account for the additional school supplies she would also require. These considerations contributed to the headache that had bothered Godo all afternoon, and made sitting beneath his tattered umbrella in the hot sun, waiting for the scarce customers, unbearable.

Matters were made even worse for Godo upon his return home, greeted as he was by a chaotic homestead—dirty pans strewn about, the children unwashed and crying, his wife

---

[5] bicycle/motorbike taxi

nowhere to be seen. He had hoped for a tasty calabash of *wimbi*[6] porridge and a warm bath, and a late visit to the brewer's compound for a tin of grain-beer to ease his headache and help lull him to sleep later that night.

It was dark by the time Adema and her brother returned from the stream.

"Did your mother not tell you where she was going, and how long she would be gone?" he asked her yet again.

"No, baba," Adema said with a shake of her head.

"Well, you will have to prepare the meal for your siblings and put them to bed," he told her.

Godo then set about locking their cow and two goats in for the night. After the evening meal of *ugali*[7] and dried *omena*[8] fried in onions and tomatoes, Adema pulled down the sleeping mats from where they were tucked away in the rafters and prepared their sleeping places. Godo lingered in the darkness of the front room. He had blown out the lamp after the children had gone to bed to conserve kerosene. As the stillness of night set in, the chickens settled in around Godo's feet, tucking their heads into their wings, and the cockroaches and rats came out of their hiding places to begin their ceaseless night-long foraging in search of food. From the inner room the children could be heard snoring softly.

Godo rose and left the hut, drawing the door shut behind him. For a while he paced around the compound, straining to hear the footsteps of his wife on the path. December had come and gone so there was not the excuse of attending

---

[6] millet
[7] maize meal, a Kenyan staple.
[8] dried sardines

late-night choir practice at the church. As for plaiting her hair—another reason she might be away—such a task was unlikely to keep her out past midnight.

He had prepared well for his wife's return—a thin guava cane broken off a tender sapling swung by his side. The nights were breezy and warm and the moon was preparing to show itself. It was a fine evening to be out with the boys. He knew that the brewer's would be brimming over with late patrons, sitting in little groups in the yard, chewing the fat of the day over a leisurely drink. He could hear villagers on the path beyond his house, either traveling to or returning from the brewer's compound. Although these men were known to him by voice, he did not wish to call out a greeting over the unkempt euphorbia hedge.

It was as the late chill set in that Rona finally returned to the compound. She hesitated at the entrance, as if she knew there was trouble waiting. Rona eyed the hut warily, the guilt evident on her face. On seeing Godo's bicycle leaning against the wall of the hut by the front entrance she started circling the hut, intending to approach from the back entrance, quite unaware that Godo was following her in the shadows. As she fiddled with the knot in her *lesso*,[9] he stepped out of the shadows like a wraith and seized her by the arm. Rona spun around with a gasp as the guava cane descended.

Within a short time, a sizeable crowd of curious onlookers had formed outside Godo's compound, drawn by Rona's shrieks.

---

[9] Cotton wrapper for women introduced by the Swahili people of the East African coast but now commonly used by rural women across the country.

"*Bayaa!* What is going on in there, do you know?" Matayo, the quail-keeper inquired of Omenda, the carpenter. "It sounds to me like someone receiving a thorough beating." The two men were on their way home from the brewer's, and had paused on the path that skirted Godo's compound.

"Godo must be disciplining his wife," said Omenda, peering through the leaves of the euphorbia hedge.

"But why should he beat her that hard? I would have thought that one or two slaps were appropriate for a misbehaving woman."

"Maybe she did something real bad."

"Godo is usually a reserved and calm chap who goes about his bicycle repairs without bothering anyone."

"Maybe the two of you should go in and lend a hand instead of just standing there," said Onzere, the miller, as he strolled up the path, joining the two men by the euphorbia hedge. "Judging by her screams, that man is surely going to kill his wife."

Onzere was right. The screams were getting louder and louder in company with the swish of the guava cane as it descended upon her back. The gathered men could see the couple clearly as they tussled in the moonlit yard outside the front door.

"You are right. Maybe we should go in and help," said Dome, a new arrival at the hedge. He assisted Onzere at the mill, and had accompanied the miller for an after-work drink.

"But is it really right for us to intervene?" asked Omenda hesitantly. "I mean, this is clearly a matter between a man and his wife, and Godo is within his rights to discipline his wife when she strays. In any case, we don't even know what it's all about."

"You are right," said Matayo with a thoughtful nod. "What if we went in and Godo, upon seeing us, decided to dash in for his machete and turned it on us?"

"I say the lot of you should be ashamed of yourselves for making lame excuses in a matter that clearly needs our intervention," said the miller, stepping into the compound. "Do you want someone to be killed before you can make up your minds?"

All four men were required to restrain Godo, who seemed intent on inflicting indelible damage on his wife.

"*Bayaa!* Have you gone mad, Godo?" the miller cried, holding the bicycle repairman by locking his elbows firmly behind him. "Is that the way a man disciplines his wife? I say, cool down, Godo. You are going to kill the woman."

"I said let go of me!" spat Godo, struggling with the beefy miller. "That woman deserves a dog's beating!"

"Oh, calm down, Godo," said Omenda, who, unlike the brave miller, was keeping his distance. He was still smarting from a kick in the shin that Godo had given him as they struggled to get the bicycle repairman off his wife. "You don't want to go to the cells now, do you?"

"And why should I go to the cells, you coward? Is it now a crime to discipline an errant wife? Have the lot of you become a bunch of women?"

"The police will surely come into this matter if you carry on like this," said the miller, holding Godo firmly in a bear hug. "*Hooo!* You call us women, do you, Godo? Well, you can hear this from my own lips. You will go to the cells this very minute, I tell you! Don't you know that these days the *serikali*[10] is different? *He-heee!* You will see fire, Godo, I tell you!"

"And that is why the lot of you see fit to come in here uninvited and threaten me in my own compound, is it? Are you now going to heap abuse on me in front of my own wife, Onzere?" demanded Godo, kicking viciously at the miller with renewed zeal. "I say, let go of me!"

The miller struggled to hook his feet over Godo's in an effort to protect himself, and the two men went tumbling to the ground, rolling in the dewy grass. It was only after Omenda and Matayo each seized one of Godo's flailing feet that the miller was finally able to sit on Godo and thereby restrain him.

It was well toward midnight when the men—with the help of three other neighbors who had been drawn out of their compounds by Rona's screams—were finally able to calm Godo. But even then it was another effort to get Rona back inside the hut with her husband.

"The man will kill me. I swear to God he will after you leave this place," she cried, hiding behind a stocky woman. "You cannot trust what he says. Can't you see it in his eyes? He is still intent on killing someone, I swear to you!"

"Godo has given us his word. This matter is settled. Or haven't you, Godo?" asked the miller, patting the silent bicycle repairman on the shoulder. Godo nodded, his gaze trained on his twitching toes. "See? Now, go inside, Rona. The matter is settled."

"No. I must hear him say it with his own lips," Rona insisted. In the bright moonlight angry welts crisscrossed her

---

[10] Swahili for "the government."

bared arms, her dress reduced to tattered strips. "I must hear it from the man himself."

"What do you say, Godo?" asked the miller in a fatherly tone. "She needs to hear your word. Go on; assure her that this is now settled."

"I say get back inside!" growled Godo. "Go inside and get to bed!"

"Now, that is the spirit," said the miller. "This is really a small matter that needn't get beyond the walls of this compound."

There was a brief scuffle later that night after the villagers had left. But unlike the earlier battle, this one was brief, lasting barely a couple of minutes. One of the neighbors heard Godo say to his wife, "You want me to take out my *nyaunyo*[11] now, is that what you want, woman?"

For a while the woman whimpered, then when Godo's voice started rising, she said, "No, no, do not take it out. I will tell you. I will tell you everything, Godo."

There followed a muffled conversation, the likes of which the neighbors could not quite hear despite straining their ears to do so. Thereafter the couple were quiet and the stillness of night returned.

It was the busy hour at the village *duka*[12] when every villager suddenly wanted to run to the shop to purchase a matchbox, or a quarter kilo of sugar, or a scoop of cooking fat for the evening meal. As usual the shopkeeper's wife had to leave

---

[11] A whip cut out of an old car tyre
[12] shop

her chores at the back of the shop and lend a hand at the counter. But even with his wife helping dispense measures of milk and kerosene at the other end, Suba, the shopkeeper, found that the queue kept increasing at his end because he kept handing back the wrong change, and had to constantly use the little calculator on the counter to get it right. These errors were uncharacteristic of Suba, who was famous for being a "walking computer" when it came to small change.

Finally Suba came to the second-to-last customer in his queue, a man who had patiently hung back to allow everyone else to get their purchases. It had now grown dark, and it was impossible to see beyond the ring of light thrown by the lantern resting on the counter. At the other end of the long scarred wooden counter Suba's wife was engaged in an argument with an elderly woman, who felt the measure splashed into her bottle was less than two shillings' worth of kerosene—even though the cost of everything was shooting through the ceiling these days.

Rona disengaged herself from the pillar on which she had been leaning and approached the counter. "Sugar and a matchbox," she said, placing ten shillings' worth of silver coins on the counter. Suba took the money and, without bothering to count it, deposited the coins in the little drawer underneath the counter. He then took the sugar scoop and measured out a kilo from the sack beneath the weighing scale. To this he added two boxes of matches, a packet of tea leaves and a sachet of curry powder. Suba then worked out the amount of Rona's change on his calculator, sucking in his lower lip in concentration.

"That will be twenty-five shillings and fifty cents in

change, is that right?" he asked, his eyes lifting from the little electronic gadget.

"That's right, Suba," said his customer with a half-smile. And in that brief second that the shopkeeper's gaze locked with that of his customer he felt his heart flip over.

"Right," he added hastily, drawing his gaze away in the manner of a schoolboy flustered by his first date. "I'll wrap your purchases for you," he added, a little nervously—reliving, as he was, the brief moment of electricity when her fingers had brushed his as he handed over the change.

After taping the old newspapers around her packages, Suba reached into the sweets jar and took out a handful. "These are for the children. My good little friends always offer to push my laden bicycle up the hill for me on my way from the market."

Rona smiled coyly and took the bundle.

Before she stepped away into the darkness, Rona glanced back and, as the shopkeeper's eyes met hers for the second time, he jerked his thumb slightly over his shoulder and gave a little wink that his wife—who was still engaged in the argument with the elderly shopper at the other end of the counter—couldn't see. It was a brief signal that anyone watching from the path wouldn't have noticed. And then Rona turned and was gone into the night, her long skirts sweeping into the darkness like the tail-fin of the mermaid the shopkeeper had painted on one of the shop pillars.

Suba leaned against the counter for a while, listening to his wife argue with the adamant customer as he pored over the faded pictures on an old newspaper page. A couple of children came up to buy sweets, lingering a while to joke with the shopkeeper as they wet the palms of their hands on their tongues and pressed them on the counter to draw the spilt grains of sugar. Soon after they left Suba rose and announced to his wife, "I am going off to see to the cattle. That boy we employed doesn't quite lock them in properly. You had better hang around for the last customers."

With a last glimpse around the well-stocked shop he collected his coat from the nail behind the door and left, struggling to get his thick arms through the narrow sleeves.

In the darkness of the path-side bushes the two lovers were a little shy of each other, as if they were meeting for the first time. They kept glancing over their shoulders, as if expecting someone to suddenly appear, even though they knew the path to the well was seldom used at this hour. They stood, holding hands, close enough to feel each other's body heat through their clothing. A shaft of moonlight stole through the tattered banana leaves overhead and fell on Rona's face, highlighting her fine features.

"Let's go," Suba said, tugging at her hand. In the darkness his eyes glowed with the hopelessness of the totally devoted.

"Uh-uh," she whispered, shaking her head. "Not today."

"But why?" he pleaded.

For answer she gazed steadily into his eyes, standing on the tips of her toes so that his warm breath caressed her face. "You haven't heard, have you?" she asked with that soft coyness that set his heart afire.

"Haven't heard what?" he asked, inching closer so that the tips of her pointed breasts brushed against his chest.

"Oh, I see you haven't," she said with a slow nod. "Well, it can't be tonight," she added with a slow shake of her head. "No, it would be too soon after."

"Just what are you talking about?" he asked, pulling her into his embrace. "Come on, you aren't changing your mind now, are you?"

"Uh-uh!" she said with a shake of the head.

"After all we've had? You don't enjoy it, is that what you are saying?"

"You know I do," she whispered, pressing herself against him. "You know I enjoy it as much as you do."

"Well, what is it then?" He passed his hands behind her shoulders and cupped her face in his hands, staring intently into her dark eyes.

"Just not today," she said, roping her arms about his waist.

"Oh, let's go," he pleaded, crushing her against him in his tight embrace. "Come on, we must go. Only tonight. I will go mad if we don't."

She knew where he meant. It was their usual rendezvous. The stack of fresh nappier grass the cowherd left behind the cattle shed for feeding the cows the following morning was softer than any bed either of them had ever lain on, and the cowherd's old sack covered with Rona's *lesso* wrap made for a perfect bedspread. They had lain on this very bed the previous night, gazing up at the stars in the night-sky as they explored each other's bodies.

"No, it can't be tonight," she said, shaking her head firmly. "It can be dangerous, believe me."

"You know you really are driving me mad," Suba said, crushing her to him, an irrepressible sense of urgency overtaking him. He had drawn up the skirt of her dress with his left hand and was stroking her warm buttock through the thin fabric of her nylon panties. "We must go today. Only today," he pleaded. As she hesitated, he tugged at his belt-buckle and unzipped his pants, letting them pool around his feet. And as he drove his naked thighs up against her warm soft flesh, he closed his eyes and a soft sigh escaped his parted lips.

But before she could answer, a figure suddenly loomed on the deserted path, having detached itself from the surrounding bushes with a rustle, and the two lovers were washed in the bright light of a six-volt flashlight.

"Oh, so it was you all the while, was it, Suba?" Godo's words shattered the stillness of the sheltered banana grove like a curse, freezing them in their tracks. "So it was you messing with my house all this while?"

Before they could turn around a deafening slap had cracked on Rona's cheek, ringing in the conspiratorial stillness like a pistol shot. It sent her reeling back, a shriek escaping her lips.

"Suba, *gooooo*...I just can't believe it!" screamed Godo. The bicycle repairman's cries roused the entire village and they appeared one by one, sleepy and disheveled on the path to the well. They paused, waiting to find out who else among their neighbors had heard the commotion, rubbing their eyes to clear them of sleep. In little gatherings they drew closer to see what was the matter. "Come and see; come and see for yourselves...*goooooo*!"

Godo, leaping at the dumbstruck shopkeeper, brandished a piece of rusty metal piping that he had carried in the sleeve of his coat, aiming for Suba's head. The shopkeeper, rooted to the spot and blinded by the glaring flashlight, swung up his arm to ward off the blow and caught it squarely on the upper arm, the resultant *thunk* suggesting a broken bone. Suba cried out, trying to regain his balance but disadvantaged by his trousers that pooled still around his feet, entangling him.

It took three strong men to disentangle Godo, who straddled the half-naked shopkeeper on the ground, pounding at him like a madman. Rona sat huddled a little distance away, screaming helplessly at the horror of the fighting men.

The trial was held at the village square two days later, conducted by the Council of Elders. Respectable clansmen from both sides had turned up to lend support to one of their own, heads carefully cocked for any discrepancy to traditional procedure in a case of this magnitude. But the lead counsel was evidently an old hand at the business, and would ensure that all proprieties were duly observed.

The court sat on the worn logs arranged in a semi-circle underneath the old fig tree where the chief usually held his weekly *baraza*.[13] The accused sat on the swept ground to one side of the semi-circle, head lowered as he listened to the proceedings. Suba cradled his injured arm, encased in thick white plaster in his lap, and drew support from his clansmen who had positioned themselves behind him. The complainant glared at Suba's bowed figure from the other end of the semi-circle, equally hemmed in by his clansmen. The woman sat on the ground a little distance away, her back turned to the court, unable to lift her head for shame. A band of young men were positioned around the court, keeping

---

[13] A formal meeting in the village at which the chief makes important announcements from the government

away the village children who attempted to have a peek.

It proved to be a difficult tussle of a case, with both sides putting up strong arguments. But everyone knew that, in the end, it was the testimony of the witnesses that would carry the day. Godo had lined up four good speakers, including the miller, Onzere. Another villager—who had been among the first to arrive at the scene of the crime—gave a lengthy, if unnecessarily graphic, description of what he had seen that left everyone in stitches. He, too, had been carefully chosen, as one who had paid through the nose for petty items at the *duka*; a man, in short, who was not the best of friends with the accused.

As the sun climbed high in the sky, the elders finally rose to consult with one another about the verdict. "The court is agreed that the accused has committed a crime," the elders' spokesman finally announced after lengthy deliberation. "And we all know the fine for breaking someone's leg.[14] As per our custom, Godo will be required to pay a cow, together with a sum of money that the complainant's side will agree on."

Early the Monday after the trial Godo was seen leaving the village, dressed in his black boots and the fine tweed coat a relative from Nairobi had bought him. He swung his walking stick jauntily by his side in the manner of someone who was going on an important journey. His daughter Adema followed behind, resplendent in her bright new school uniform, her hair shaved. Bringing up the rear was Godo's wife, bearing Adema's new metal trunk on her head.

---

[14] A euphemism for having a love affair with someone else's wife

28

THE STRONGER HAND

I was a master brewer by the time I was nine, as was expected in my family, and since no one in their right mind would employ a three-and-a-half-foot midget anyway, this suited me fine. Growing up in the remote district of Apac, Uganda, my sights weren't exactly set on brewing when I came of age. I dreamed of spreading my wings—like the buzzards that flocked the local slaughtery whenever there was a kill—and taking to the air. It was clear in my mind even as I helped my Uncle Papa, who was charged with my upbringing, out with the brown lumps of jaggery[15] at the brewery deep in the valley on the lower side where the town's sludge flowed. My destiny lay among the clouds where the birds soared, not hustling droop-eyed drunks for their last shilling in dingy shebeens. I had decided that as soon as I turned eighteen, I would present myself at the nearest army recruitment office to be trained as a helicopter pilot. This, I knew, was what the gods had intended for me.

On the cusp of my seventeenth year, when a recruitment exercise was advertised near our home—and against the wishes of my family—I made good my burning desire. I recall the army officer bending down to look me over, a wry smile twitching at the corners of his hard-set mouth. He was a tall, dark Dinka from the Sudan border, and he possessed

---

[15] Raw brown sugar made from crushed cane juice, predominately used in a brewery

the contemptible gleam in his bloodshot eyes that the Goliaths of this world reserve for the Davids.

"You really want to join the army, young man, eh?" he asked, bemused.

"Yessah!" I bellowed, pushing my puny chest out as far as it would go. I was conscious of the bemused side glances of the other hopeful recruits waiting tensely in line.

"Well, that is quite ambitious," mused the officer. "And you might just pass the tests, judging from the burning ambition in your eyes."

We recruits had stripped off our shirts for the physical examination; those of us not in shorts rolled our trouser legs up over our knees to expose what we were made of. The officer examined me carefully, taking particular interest in my well-toned calf muscles, as a butcher might size up the morning delivery of carcasses.

"You look fit enough to me," the officer proclaimed at length. "But, my little man, there is *one* qualification that you could never hope to pass."

Perhaps one of the cruelest things to say to a pigmy is that they are short. I felt the blood rush to my ears as the tip of the officer's hard cane softly but firmly pushed me out of the line. I walked with my head held high, even as the sniggers sounded behind me, out of the recruitment center. It seemed that my presence had done nothing but provide comic relief to an otherwise dour exercise.

That afternoon I got very drunk on my uncle's brew before sneaking into a grass-thatched hut to screw one of my uncle's concubines. Later, after copious vomiting, I slept through my heavy hangover. When I awoke, my mind was made up. I was leaving. My uncle had, for some time, been urging me to leave for Nairobi, where we had relatives who were doing quite well for themselves. Our family brewing empire had so spread its influence over the years so that we now had a presence in virtually every city in East Africa. It was time for me to set up my own operation.

Our Apac home was getting crowded, but my uncle would not tell me so openly. I had come to the south after fleeing the violence of a LRA-NRA exchange in the northern town of Gulu. My parents both fell victims to the gunfire, and my sister had been captured by Kony's goons—doubtless she was someone's sex-slave in the bush. I was the only one of my nuclear family to escape the brutality and, for this reason, my uncle had felt obliged to keep me on until the opportunity arose for me to leave.

I accepted the tickets from my uncle and reported early at the Akamba bus station in Kampala the following Monday. After I had boarded and was on my way, I reflected on my uncle's words and the bundle of letters—written in pencil in halting vernacular on grubby papers pulled out of old school notebooks—for me to take to our relations.

"You will be in safe hands, Apuka, believe me," the old man had said. "Our people there will show you the way more than I ever could here in Apac. I know the Papa in Nairobi—he is a good man and will set you up well. You will make a fine brewer with a business of your own—for was it not I who honed your hand?"

While I knew what I was leaving behind, I had little idea of what awaited me. I would miss the barefoot easy-to-lay girls of Apac and the older women with hand-chiseled gaps between their front teeth who knew how to time their husbands' return. I would miss their warm thighs and their full breasts in my palm on a starlit night. I would miss the gonorrhea and syphilis, too, which, like a tail on a dog, naturally came after in these matters—afflictions which the village healer aptly resolved with several bottles of bitter leaf extract. I would miss the hills that were shrouded in mist in the mornings and tinted gold at sunset. I would miss the easy, carefree life and the ringing laughter; the smell of cattle and the fresh air of the fields; the taste of fried sun-dried white ants eaten with *ugali* and *matooke*,[16] and the pot-cooked meals that only Apac women knew how to make. For even though I had never been to a big city like Nairobi, I felt that I was migrating to a place where people burrowed like rats through narrow spaces.

My people received me at the station and we drove off in a battered Bedford taxi, one operated by another of my uncles on the Lunga Lunga route. As we wove our way slowly down the crowded thoroughfares of the strange town, my earlier fears were proven correct. I had never seen such an early rush as that on Tom Mboya Street. The pace of the serious-looking people on the sidewalk was dizzying, as was the bumper-to-bumper traffic, the screeching brakes of reckless drivers, and the deafening car music. The streets were crowded with foul-mouthed cab drivers, with their elbows hooked over their windows and their jaws working furiously at lumps of *qhat*[17] like some sort of sacrament required to

---

[16] Boiled or fried green bananas or plantains; a staple in Uganda
[17] A twig grown in the Kenyan highlands that when chewed acts as a mild stimulant, particularly popular among the Somali community of

stay awake on the job. It was an alien world.

We followed Valley Road out of town and wound between groves of soot-colored trees where fine red-tiled houses were tucked, surrounded by smooth patches of lawn. I wondered why such beautiful homes were walled in by six-foot walls, topped with coils of shiny razor wire. I reflected upon the simple thatched huts of Apac that were enclosed by a low-trimmed, waist-high hedge. We passed Yaya Centre and the Valley Arcade, and I watched as the elegant houses started to give way to the less-pleasant dwellings of Kawangware.

Again, there were hordes of people crowding the side-walk, and the air had thickened with a warm putrefaction. The rickety tin-and-timber kiosks, built over open sewers, leaned into the road, their dirty lace curtains flapping to and fro on the breeze. We left the main road and wound our way through the narrow alleyways of the Congo slum toward Uncle's house, with frequent stops for a bony dog or a pot-bellied child who were in no hurry.

After my arrival I bathed, ate, and rested before being escorted to my uncle's club in Congo for a drink. Congo came alive at night in such a way that only those who lived there could truly appreciate. While much of the city congregated in the hip, up-market venues to unwind after their day, the Kawangware residents sought out the delights of Congo. The patrons of Congo's nightlife consisted of guards who worked in the private homes in the neighboring suburb of Lavington, as well as gardeners, houseboys, plumbers, electricians, house-helps and all manner of handymen who derived a living in one way or another from the affluent residential

northern Kenya and among urban youth

areas bordering Kawangware. They found employment in lowly jobs that paid just enough to keep their shirts on their backs; and they would descend upon the town at the end of their work day in dust-blown droves, intending to drown their sorrows in Congo's tins and plastic tubs before retiring, staggering and bleary-eyed, to their abodes in the darkened tin city.

The tin-walled shebeens were arranged haphazardly around a man-made lake that shimmered like a mirror in the fading rays of the sun. At the fringe of the lake a four-piece band belted out tribal music from a set of tin drums, a lyre, and several homemade electric guitars wired to an amplifier and loudspeaker and powered by an old car battery. A handful of their fans were just warming up to the act, shaking a leg here and snapping a finger there as they drank from the rusty tins. A little distance away, one of the shebeen attendants tipped a huge sooty drum full of waste water from the brewery into the frothing lake. Another staggered to the edge of the lake, unzipped his trousers, and sent a jet of steaming urine arching above the shimmering lake. At the far end of the lake, where a church group had erected a striped tent, children stripped off their school uniforms and jumped into the lake, sending a flock of wild ducks that had been idling on the rippling surface scuttling into the thick marsh that ringed the perimeter.

I was enjoying the easy camaraderie of the place and my earlier misgivings had evaporated. Uncle Kuka, who I soon understood to be the Papa in the place, had the stocky women refill my tin from the special brew reserved for his special guests. One sip of the stuff, and I could lay it bare on my tongue layer by layer. My master brewer taste-buds could discern all the shortcuts Uncle Kuka had taken, as well as the various industrial chemicals they had employed to aid the fermentation process along. This was the city, and cutting corners was inevitable in the pursuit of profit, but I knew that if you attempted to sell this swill in Apac, you would not see a single customer the following day.

"We have heard a lot about you, cousin Apuka. *Karibu bwana!*"[18] said most of my relations as Papa made the introductions, pumping my hand in the customary manner—the left hand clasped around the other's right bicep while the two right hands clasped in a shoulder-wrenching shake that lasted the better part of a minute. Uncle Kuka, or Papa as he was popularly known, made sure I was introduced to everyone that mattered in the business. As expected, it turned out that most of my clansmen fared no better than I on matters vertical, making up for the shortfall with excellent musculature and wit—I was quickly aware of the special talents amongst my kin. The majority of our clansmen were short, reaching approximately five feet, and a handful of us were pygmies, for which there was an explanation.

For generations, our clan kept a little stock and did a little farming, but our primary income was established by trade, and this was the reason for the old tribal joke that "money ran in our veins." Our clan operated as smalltime vendors, selling measures of cloth, spices, and leather products from door to door; or, they sold *mitumba*[19] at open-air markets, or acted as loan sharks, giving the banks cutthroat competition

---

[18] Swahili for "welcome, sir"
[19] used clothes

for the lower echelons of the money-lending business. Senior members of the clan dealt in gemstones, which entailed both greater rewards and greater risks. The most familiar way of making a living for our clan, however, was in the brewing business. For years the government had sought to control and legitimize the brewing industry and would hunt down small-time bootleg dealers. Our clan forebears had long understood that brewing was a goldmine comparable only to the church, witchcraft, and prostitution. Brewing, like witchcraft, could thrive underground, especially in a big city like Nairobi.

I am told that one of the reasons why our clan women are so hardy is that they have always traditionally served us as carriers, traveling even into the Congo to trade. The most credible explanation for the scattered pygmies in our midst was that our women had had intercourse with the Twa during their long absences in the vast Congo.

But then, this was not to say that we—the special talents— were despised or looked down upon by the clan. For we were walking computers when it came to accounting, and the clan relied on our wily foresight when it came to speculation. For just like ants, we could predict a rainy day with uncanny accuracy. We were special. It was for this reason that when I was introduced to my pygmy cousins, Babu and Mbiko—who ran the show across the valley in Kangemi—our handshakes were from the heart, like blood brothers meeting after a long estrangement.

Later, as the place filled, we settled into a long drinking and dancing session by the lake, our faces lit by the fiery glow of the fading sun. As the night progressed, Papa, reappearing by my side, asked whether I possessed sufficient energy for some late-night entertainment. A slim brown girl—with an artificial gap between her front teeth, just as we liked it—stood, looking eager, by Papa's side. Papa needn't have bothered. I had already made my own overture toward a stocky waitress who, like most women in my life, was eager to discover whether I was a "man" or a "boy." She had fallen immediately into my spider's web. As the evening wound up and we danced to the progressively vulgar lyrics of the four-piece band, I no longer felt any regret about traveling to Nairobi—I was home, in good company, and we, a bunch of crafty dwarves, were running the entire show.

The following day Papa took me to the local police station to introduce me to the OCS.[20] I had dressed that morning in a brown suede jacket that I found draped on a chair by my bedside. In the inner pocket, I discovered a fat brown envelope. Sitting on the hard bench in the police station, with Papa to my right and Mbiko to the left, I felt an icy sweat of apprehension snaking slowly down my side. I have never learnt to be comfortable around those in authority.

It was to be a short meeting. Papa formally presented me as the special representative of our other Papa across the border, a rep who had come to take care of the latter's business in Nairobi. The OCS, a dark sweaty fellow with a tummy that wouldn't allow him to bend over without a fart, eyed me carefully, perhaps trying to assess whether I would fit in with his own end of the business. In the end, with the fat manila envelope tucked safely in his pocket, the OCS's face crumbled into an awkward grin and he rose, pumping

[20] Officer Commanding Station

my shoulder in a mighty hug.

The rest of the day was spent in a tour of the clan brewery, deep in the Mau Mau valley that separated Kawangware from Kangemi. I was introduced to the rest of the clan, who worked the sooty drum-ensemble that fed the city's hooch industry. Other than grain beer, the Nairobi branch also distilled a modified version of the *waragi*[21] we brewed in Apac; a gin which borrowed from the local *chang'aa*[22] and was laced with additives to give the Nairobi customers more kick in their tipple. This gin was predominately sold in small joints that dotted the ghetto like hydra heads and which were mostly operated by our clan women. It was a tight set-up that left the local drunks with little choice but to deposit their Caesar's coin into our purse.

I opened my own joint the following month with a loan my Uganda Papa had sent by an Akamba Bus courier and the assistance of the clan. The first month, I learned the scene and became acquainted with the regular drunks. The stocky woman, with whom I had shared my bed and my confidences, helped me assemble a working team. Her name was Ida, and she made it known in Congo that she would be taking care of me—as if I needed taking care of. In Apac, the men were responsible for the brewing, while the women ran the shebeens. The brewing industry in Nairobi operated similarly, although the men were obliged to hang around the bar during business hours, just in case some rough characters refused to pay up. Shebeen fights were also commonplace, especially around mid-month when the guards received their

---

[21] A harsh gin popular in Uganda.

[22] A home-made liquor popular in Kenya.

advance pay, and at month's-end, when everyone else was loaded. This was debt-collection time, when women working the counter needed to collect IOUs from those who had taken goods on credit during the month. While we were very persuasive when pursuing a debt, we can turn real nasty real fast when push comes to shove—which can happen quite often in a business that skirts the law. And so, whenever a call for help is sent by any member of the clan over a business matter, you can be certain that the entire brotherhood will turn up to lend a hand. And we do not forget old scores; it is said we have the memory of an elephant. This was one of the many comforts of belonging to the clan—the knowledge that if something untoward were to happen to you, you would be avenged.

The first year of business was a loss. I set out ten drums every morning, and had barely sold half of them by the end of the day. Residents had yet to warm to me, and the club owner across the street, Kaka, had what we called in business a "stronger hand," cutting me from below the knees. Although, strictly speaking, he was of the clan, and a pygmy to boot, Kaka was of the minority Wambilangya family, who were slowly emerging as our rivals in business. The Wambilangyas were closely related to the Bukusus from across the border, and had been dismissed in Apac as "fringe cousins." I had little imagined that this far from home, these differences would amount to much. I was wrong.

As I watched the customers flock to Kaka's club, it slowly became apparent to me just why my Apac Papa had sent me to Nairobi. I was the fire-forged piece that was to put a spanner in the works of the ambitious Wambilangyas—no doubt these were the instructions I had carried for my Nairobi Papa in those grubby letters that I had brought with me. I tried all the usual tricks. Normally, after we had completed our daily brewing, a clan elder came to "doctor" the brew before we opened for business. Each family had a specific elder assigned to this delicate, closely guarded duty in exchange for a token of the takings. This had been our custom since the beginning of time, and we continued its practice wherever we emigrated.

One evening, after the club had been closed for the night, I had my ten drums ready for the old man to bestow his blessings, having previously discussed with him my predicament with Kaka. At the appointed midnight hour, the *mzee*[23] knocked on the back door and I let him in. I watched him from the corner of my eye—for typically he preferred to be left alone with the brew—as he extracted a small dead field mouse, with black stripes running across its back, from his shoulder bag. It was the kind of mouse that could be found on dumps and in the hedgerows surrounding the wealthier quarters of Nairobi. Next he produced, crumpled into a ball, the soiled knickers of a menstruating woman. Where he had gotten that was a mystery that only he knew. The old man worked the drums with a sense of indifference, and I felt, with a sense of unease, that I was on a losing streak; and my instincts were seldom wrong.

Then, before removing the most revered object from his worn bag, the *mzee* gave me a stern glance and bade me leave the room. I knew this mysterious object to be the special stirrer that every brewing family invests in, and which singly

---

[23] Swahili for "old man"

determines the direction of the business. There had been a moment of carelessness on the part of the Apac *mzee*, and I had seen the stirrer gripped between his bony, gnarled fingers. And so I waited while the *mzee* went to work on my investment.

The following day, I opened as usual and left my hired hands to conduct the business. As anticipated, sales continued to be meagre, little better than the day before. I opened early and the usual crowd of nighttime workers arrived in twos and threes. But later in the day, after Kaka had opened his doors, the usual pattern played itself out. One by one my customers ambled over, sometimes to greet a friend they had seen on the other side of the street, or to take a sample of Kaka's daily brew. They never came back, despite the fact that I had invested heavily in "pimping" up my club, with a 42-inch LCD TV and a powerful stereo system; I even had plans to acquire pay TV in order to cash in on the English soccer craze sweeping through the town. And this was how the ungrateful idiots paid me back!

I had never taken failure lightly and quitting was unacceptable. As I nursed my losses, Kaka was smiling all the way to the bank. I watched him mingle with the customers—his clean-shaven pate shiny with sweat, his single cut-glass earring shining in the dim light, a wide smile permanently frozen on his broad face—and I felt a furious jealousy well up from within me, and, for the first time, I thought of employing other means to get what I wanted.

Whenever men make the mistake of courting one of our women—who I admit are most attractive—we always encourage them in their amorous pursuits. This is one way in which we have spread our tentacles. The lovesick man probably never finds out that he has been marked from the start, that we are waiting in the wings for him to sow his wild oats. Thereafter he becomes one of us, whether he likes it or not. In this manner, we have obtained a number of "clansmen" from the highest echelons of government, from the judiciary and the legislature, and many a one from the clergy. This method of recruitment is the secret ace that we keep carefully up our collective sleeves, and one which we use only when absolutely necessary.

I knew of two influential "relations" in neighboring Lavington. One of them was married to a girl from our village, and she happened to know my Apac Papa well; her folks had worked at our brewery before migrating to Nairobi. The other had been ensnared by his city wife, a pygmy like me, who had set her claws so deep that her husband had practically abandoned his family upcountry. Naturally, due to our foreshortened height, she had become my special sister. The first fellow was in a position to cause mild trouble in regard to licenses and other legalities required to do business in Nairobi. The other was a big shot in the Public Health Department. It was easy to have someone block the makeshift sewage lines serving Kaka's pub and cause the stuff to flow back inside on a crowded day; alternatively I could arrange to have dead sewer rats dropped in the beer drums and then have the health inspector's van turn up before anyone knew what was going on. Attractive as the two avenues were, in the end I decided that a more permanent solution was required.

After closing the doors that evening, I paid Papa a visit at his club. He had a private room in the back where he usually retired when he did not wish to be disturbed, whether to run a check on the business records, to meet with a business partner, or entertain a woman. I was accompanied by my good friend, Mbiko. Together, we found Papa lolling on the overstuffed sofa smoking weed, his head resting in the lap of a curvaceous dark woman called Serah, their faces lit by the glow of a fourteen-inch TV set.

"Ah, *karibu*, my two favourite uncles, Apuka and Mbiko!" he said, sitting up. "I've just been thinking about you and our business. Come, take a seat."

Papa ushered us to the easy chairs and snapped on a switch that lit a pink overhead bulb. A half-empty bottle of Borzoi sat on the table together with two glasses and an overflowing ashtray. Papa's woman brought two clean glasses over from the cabinet.

For a while we spoke of politics and the latest news from home, working our way down the Borzoi bottle. Papa's woman slapped together a delicious meal of fried beef and *matooke*—just the way it was made back home. I found it amusing that as we partook of the finer things, our customers swallowed freshly pressed sisal juice, menses, and embalming fluid. But then it occurred to me that the Borzoi, too, might have its own secret ingredients known only to its maker.

Papa's woman interrupted the meal to usher in our tribal *mzee*, who had just arrived from his day-long jaunts.

"Ah, there you are!" said Papa cheerfully. "I and my little uncles here were just skirting around the business problem I was telling you about. It is good you came."

The *mzee*, looking troubled, washed his hands and joined us at table, placing his bag with its precious cargo gingerly beside his chair where he could keep an eye on it. As the discussion became increasingly grim, Papa sent Mbiko to fetch three more of our uncles who were supervising the business outside. As the night progressed, the discussion turned from the broad needs of the clan to the particular difficulties of our family. The Wambilangyas were not only wrecking havoc with business in Congo, but were starting to infiltrate other slums around the city where we maintained a presence. We were informed, by one of our uncles who had kept his ear to the ground, of their exploits in Mathare, Mukuru and Kibera, where they had the Kundos by the neck. And with every revelation, all eyes turned to our tribal *mzee*.

"We all know what the problem is," said Papa, summing up the matter. "And we should not pretend about it. The Wambilangyas, for some reason, have the stronger hand." In other circumstances, saying this in front of our tribal *mzee* would have been high treason punishable by a heavy fine, or even banishment. But these were clearly not ordinary times. In any case, Papa and the *mzee* were of generally the same age, both revered elders, and Papa had the advantage of being host, which permitted him some liberties. The *mzee*'s heavily lined face remained lowered, sagging jowls working pensively, his cross-eyed gaze trained on a point on the floor.

"We have a problem; on that, we are agreed," Papa continued. "And unless we find a solution, the Wambilangyas will eclipse us."

In the course of the tense and lengthy discussion that followed, Mbiko and I more than once inadvertently offended the discredited tribal *mzee* by looking him in the eye. But our carelessness was excused, thanks in part to the second bottle of Borzoi that Papa had produced from the drinks cabinet. By the time we were ready to leave, the club had emptied, save for the few drunks who had passed out on the floor, and who would spend the remainder of the night locked up inside with the guards. As we made our way home through the darkened alleys, we came to a decision.

ॐ

The opportune moment presented itself six weeks later, when the news came that Kaka's teenage cousin had been killed by muggers at Mau Mau Bridge on his way from school late one evening. Whether by accident or design, only the perpetrators could tell. The boy had lived with his mother at the back of the *chang'aa* den she ran in Gichagi, Kangemi. As was the custom, the entire clan was expected to help organize the funeral. Unlike other migrant tribes in the city, whenever a clan member died we held a fundraiser to cover the cost of transporting the body home—in this case, to Uganda. The roots of our clan were firmly entrenched in Uganda, and custom demanded that the dead be laid to rest among their forebears, even if they were so far away as London and Johannesburg.

It was a drizzly Friday night, and the fourth and last day of our night funeral meetings. The fundraiser had been success-ful; one of the deceased's uncles had donated a minibus that he operated as a *matatu*[24] on Route 46, and we now needed only cash for the fuel, coffin, and other minor expenses. The close family members would travel with the body on the *matatu* hearse, with the rest of the attendants using public

---

[24] A shared public shuttle van/bus popular in Kenyan cities

45

means of transportation. We secured the necessary travel documents, thanks to our strategically placed "relation" in the Immigration Department. The body was to be collected the following day from the City Mortuary and the cortège intended to set off at sunset.

We had lit a bonfire outside the block of tin shacks where the boy had lived, and around which we had conducted our meetings. On that last day of our gatherings, the *chang'aa* had flown freely, and by the time the sun began to rise in the eastern sky, everyone had curled up in their long night-coats, sleeping. I rose from my comfortable wicker chair and walked to a bush to take a leak. As I settled back in my place and prepared to light a cigarette in the smouldering embers, Kaka, who slept next to me, stirred and opened his eyes.

"What time is it, cousin, do you know?"

I glanced at my cheap quartz clock. "Almost five. Ten minutes to. Why?"

"I was wondering if it was light enough to set off back to Kawangware. People should be up and about by now—those who need to report early for work."

Glancing toward the east, I said, with repressed excitement, "You are right, Kaka. There should be people on the road by now. It should be safe enough to cross the valley. Do you want to go to bed?"

"Me?" said Kaka with a laugh. "Oh no, I can't sleep right now. I need to chase money, *bwana*! I was thinking of opening the club earlier as I need to attend to some business at the bank in the afternoon."

I had spent considerable time in Kaka's company these past four days—gathering wood for the bonfire and assisting him with organizational tasks—and we had fallen into an easy comradeship.

"Well, if that's the case, then why don't we get on our way?" I said smoothly, glancing casually to my left. "Our business here is completed, and I might as well get a little sleep in my own bed before reporting for business."

Kaka rose and stretched, yawning into his fist. "I wonder who else is ready to leave?" he said loudly, glancing around at the sleeping men. I glanced to my left, where Mbiko was curled tightly in his jacket, his chin tucked deep into the raised collar.

"Hey, Mbiko, let's get on our way," I said, shaking him softly. "It is dawn." Mbiko grunted and rolled over, his eyes still tightly closed. I tried Papa, seated a little distance away, but he turned slightly in his chair and snored even louder.

"Oh, leave them," said Kaka, reaching for my cigarette. "Let's go. The two of us will be fine." He checked his flashlight and machete, ensuring they were tucked in place inside his jacket, before setting off into the grey dawn in the direction of the valley, dragging at the stub of cigarette. I glanced casually around as I followed him, my heart going pit-a-pat in my chest with mounting excitement. I was certain that not a soul saw us leave.

Kaka walked briskly, and I had to hurry to keep up with him. We made our way into the valley toward Mau Mau Bridge. Twice I tripped and Kaka had to wait for me.

"You know, you should eat more carrots, cousin," Kaka joked. "A man needs to have good eyesight, especially in the dark."

As we began the climb toward Kawangware, after crossing

Mau Mau Bridge, the grey dawn suddenly burst into life. We had just passed the Nissen hut—meant to serve as a police patrol post, but which had long been abandoned by cops on the night beat—when figures suddenly appeared like phantoms on the road ahead. A flashlight shone briefly before being switched off. Kaka stopped, tense, and I fell back as three figures emerged from either side of the road.

"He…" Kaka started to say, reaching into the folds of his jacket. I heard a sharp whizzing sound before a blow struck Kaka just above the ear, knocking him off his feet. Two of the figures grabbed him before he fell to the ground and dragged him into the Nissen hut. Kaka struggled against our efforts to restrain him; three of us lent our weight to keep him down. I felt the smooth handle of a hacksaw being slipped into my hand.

"Remember your lessons, *kijana*…[25] He *must* look you in the eye as you do it," whispered the coarse voice of Papa. "That is the only way it will be stronger. Now, don't mess this up."

Kaka summoned all the energy in his ox-like body and gave a mighty heave; two of us pinning him down were thrown into the wall of the tin hut. But, like canines that were drawn by the smell of blood, they bounced back and knocked him down before he could rise to his feet. A solid punch connected with Kaka's solar plexus, causing the wind to rush out of him like a punctured balloon. It was only with Papa sitting squarely on his chest, Mbiko holding his thighs, and Babu pinning his shins that he was finally stilled. Someone produced a piece of cloth and Kaka was quickly

---

[25] Swahili for "young man"

gagged. His dark face was slick with sweat, his horrified eyes like white balls popping out of his skull. Poor Kaka—his goose was cooked.

I glanced outside to see if anyone had heard the crash. Confirming there was no one on the road I went to work. Squatting above Kaka, the *mzee* switched on a flashlight, and I gripped the handle of the tiny hacksaw firmly in my hand, forcing my eyes to meet Kaka's.

I am still haunted by the sickening sound of the saw working its way through the quivering bone and the distant voice of Papa filling my head…

"Good… very good—just like a surgeon. A youthful hand for a youthful hand…just *perfect!* I always knew you were the strong one. Your other Papa, too. Turns out we were right. And you know what? You've just bought your ticket to succeed me as the next Papa when I retire. You have earned it, boy."

After we had collected our gory trophy, we finally allowed Kaka to breathe his last, aided by a forceful machete blow. Soon after, a van that had been hidden in the path-side bushes backed up to the hut, its lights off. We loaded the body and clambered inside quickly, acutely conscious of the breaking dawn. As the van sped away, someone put a bottle of Borzoi to my lips. I never needed liquor so badly—before or since.

The body, discovered on Waiyaki Way just before Uthiru later that day, had been flattened by a twenty-four-wheeler cargo truck. The second funeral that week was somber, and all the Wambilangyas were in attendance. No one was fooled—their elders had evidently pieced together all the particulars of our crime, but we were not worried. This night-time ambush was strictly an internal affair. No one was going to say a word, and any police investigations were guaranteed to hit a brick wall. Nonetheless, we were quite aware that this was not the end of the matter, and that we had only bought ourselves a little time. The Wambilangyas would bide their time before they made their own move. It was the custom.

SHIKWE AND ANDATI'S ASSIGNMENT

Shikwe walked slowly down the narrow path, swinging his load of millet from one shoulder to the other and chewing a thick stalk of brown sugarcane he had found by the stream. Andati followed close behind, carrying his own bundle of maize, which would be used to "clean" the mill after Shikwe had ground his millet. It was Andati's turn to eat the upper end of the sugarcane, which had less sugar in it.

"Shikwe, I heard Mother saying that Uncle Mukolwe is coming tomorrow," said Andati.

"Yeah, I heard it too," said Shikwe, his brow creasing.

"I hope he doesn't make it. Maybe the bus from Busia will stall or something."

"Or the bridge will overflow and the bus will have to turn back to spend the night in Bungoma."

The boys had never pretended affection for their uncle. Indeed, they became visibly tense every time he stopped in after inspecting his business in Busia, en route to his home in Shianda. Uncle Mukolwe's fingers seemed perpetually itching to slap or pinch someone for doing something wrong.

"I wonder why he has to stop by all the time," Shikwe groused. "Can't he just go on the rest of the way home?"

"Perhaps it is the prospect of having a chicken slaughtered for him," said Andati with a cheeky laugh, wiping cane juice from his chin with the back of his hand. "If there is one thing that old man is fond of, it is chicken. He can finish

51

a whole mountain of *ugali* if served with stewed chicken!"

It was often hard to tell the two boys apart, although the close observer might judge Andati to be slightly taller and leaner than his brother. Their faces were both dark and lit up in the same way when they laughed, their front teeth white and shiny against their black gums. The boys were always together. They shared a desk at the village school, slept on the same mat in the little boys' hut next to the cattle pen, and wore the same clothes—oversize faded blue jinja shirts that hung to their knees, and unbuttoned epaulettes that bounced up and down. The boys' shirt tails almost covered their identical khaki shorts, worn to a mesh at the seat.

"I wonder why Father insists on Uncle spending the night in our hut," said Shikwe, stopping to poke his big toe at a tuft of dusty grass by the path-side where a lizard had just dashed for safety.

"You mean you don't know why?" Andati asked, with a cheeky grin. "It is because he farts in his sleep, that's why."

Shikwe laughed until tears filled his eyes and ran down his cheeks. He always found Andati's perspective amusing.

For a while the boys walked on in silence, shifting their loads from one shoulder to the other as they chewed the sugarcane. Their bare feet, wet from crossing the muddy stream, had started to dry in the hot afternoon sun, leaving grey muddy streaks caked upon their wiry legs. Flies buzzed around the welts their mother's old razor had left on their clean-shaven scalps, the skin moist from the long climb. They followed a narrow path through the sugar fields, a route shorter than the main murram road.

"What is that smoke over there?" Shikwe asked, pointing

in the distance to where a thick column of dark smoke rose slowly at the edge of the cane field.

"Must be someone burning their cane," Andati answered, following his brother's gaze.

"I wish it was close to our village."

"Why?"

"I like the taste of burnt cane."

"Ha! Not me," said Andati. "I'd rather have fresh river cane any time."

While the villagers assumed the boys to be brothers, Shikwe and Andati were not, in fact, related by blood. When the boys were both still very young, Andati had come to live with Shikwe's family from his own village of Matungu. Andati's father, apparently—or so their aunt had told them—had stepped on an abandoned trap while hunting in the bush. Although his companions had managed to extract his foot from the rusty jaws of the trap and carried him home, his foot had never healed, despite the herbal concoctions applied by the village herbalist. By the time they decided to take Andati's father to the mission hospital in Mumias, the whole leg had become gangrenous and had to be amputated. This decision was of little use to Andati's father, who, the day before the scheduled amputation, slipped into a coma and died in his sleep.

Andati's mother, left on her own, had been unable to provide for Andati and his two sisters. The day her husband died, she took her pot to the well and never returned. Shikwe's father, hearing of these unfolding events, brought Andati to live with them, while the boy's two sisters went to live with an aunt in Mwitoti.

Shikwe and Andati knew that the latter's mother had married again, to a man in the neighboring village, as his second wife. Her new husband, being wealthy, had opened a vegetable stall for her at the market in Mumias. Andati's mother, Auma, had secretly visited her son, told him about her vegetable stall, and invited him to visit her there whenever they stopped in at their Uncle Abdulrahman's butcher shop in Mumias. Andati had slipped away to visit his mother's stall several times since; on the last visit she had given him a bundle of yams and simsim, which the boys shared as they walked back to the village.

The boys knew never to speak about these secret meetings, particularly in front of Shikwe's father. They seldom talked of Andati's mother when they were alone, either; her remarriage made them both a little uncomfortable.

"I wish Father sends us to Mumias soon," said Andati. "The mangoes we saw last time must have ripened by now." Guava and mango trees grew wild and lush in the old town cemetery, which the boys always passed on the way to their uncle's shop.

"Maybe we should think of something to persuade him," said Shikwe, his mouth watering at the thought of the juicy, sweet mangoes. "What about we cut the tether of the big bull so that he sends us for a replacement? It should be child's play rubbing it against a rock so that it weakens and breaks."

"That is a good idea," Andati agreed.

"Well, let's work on it tomorrow after school, then. I can almost taste those mangoes!"

A sizeable crowd of village children had gathered at the posho mill when the boys arrived. Shikwe poured his load of maize on the mesh tray vacated by a girl before him and started shifting it up and down with his hands. Andati, ambling over to the flour-encrusted mesh wire window, looked inside and grinned at the miller. The miller, snatching up a piece of maize cob, threw it playfully at Andati before resuming his work.

The miller's old bicycle leaned against the shop pillar, its rusty mudguards held in place with twisted wire over patched tyres. The cracked leather saddle, perched at a tired angle, was shiny with constant use, and bare metal spokes stuck out where rubber pedals used to be.

Andati was tempted to seize the bike and take off down the village path. But the miller, wary of boys with similar intentions, had chained it securely to the shop pillar. The old Diamond padlock, Andati knew, could be easily coaxed open with a twisted length of wire.

Massive tractors trundled past the posho mill, hauling trailers bulging with cut cane, destined for the sugar factory in Mumias. Occasionally, a *matatu* puttered along the road, crammed full of goods and passengers. It paused long enough to disgorge a passenger or two at the bus stop, before roaring away, leaving a trail of dust and black diesel smoke in its wake. Up and down the lone street of the little market, villagers went about their business, haggling over a fowl or measuring out a tin of grain.

Andati rummaged in his bag and found a tightly knotted cloth bundle buried in the millet. Coaxing the knot loose with his teeth, Andati unwrapped the bundle and handed over the grubby coins to the mill owner, who dozed on his desk beside the weighing scale.

"That is millet, right?" asked the mill owner, waking from his drowsy slumber at the clink of coins. He peered with bloodshot eyes into Andati's bag. Everyone knew the mill owner, a squat and surly man, favored the fiery *chang'aa* liqueur sold in the shack behind the mill. "Do you have the maize to clean the mill?"

"I am with him," Andati piped up.

The ill-tempered mill owner dug one thick hand into the bulging patch pocket on his tunic and counted Shikwe's grubby coins with the other, inspecting several that were nicked and twisted from the playing of poker. Visibly unhappy, he returned the fistful of coins to his pocket and ambled out the back entrance, a cheerless whistle playing on his thick lips.

The boys waited for Andati's turn to grind his corn. The miller, a wiry little man named Sudi, who had a permanent squint from smoking cheap Rooster cigarettes, was beating the khaki chute attached to the flour spout, shaking out any remaining millet flour before pouring Shikwe's maize in to "clean up" the mill.

"How would the two of you boys like to own a dog?" he asked suddenly, pulling on the stub of cigarette he was smoking.

"A dog?" asked Shikwe, perplexed. He knew that the miller liked to make fun, and was not sure if he was serious.

"Yes, a dog. You know about my old black bitch, don't you?"

"Sure," said Andati. "Isn't that the skinny one with long nipples that hang down almost to the ground?"

"Ah! So you boys know the dog! Well, she gave birth to a sizeable litter recently, as you well know. And now I have so many puppies running all over the place, I just don't know what to do with them. As you might know, the mill owner is one mean fellow who barely pays me enough to keep the shirt on my back. You know, I got an offer to go and work for some people who are opening a new mill in Ekero."

"I know of the new mill," said Shikwe. "I heard my father discussing it with someone the other day."

"Is it?" said Sudi, looking interested.

"Yes, I heard them too," said Andati. "All the villagers have been talking about the new mill."

"Well, the new mill will have four imported brand new engines—a far cry from this noisy old wreck. The Ekero mill was financed by a number of merchants who want to dominate the milling business, not just in this area but in neighboring districts as well. And I cannot lie to you boys, I am itching to work there. I have heard that the Ekero mill will take orders from as far away as Kisumu! I tell you, it is just the place I'd like to be. And the owners of this new mill know that I will bring my customers with me," Sudi confided. "Everyone here knows that I am the best miller, and that my customers would certainly follow me to the new place when word gets around that I have changed jobs."

The miller took a long drag from his cigarette, a self-satisfied smile playing on his chapped lips. "But in the meantime, as I wait for the new mill to open, I still have to put food on the table. In short, boys, what I am saying is that I cannot feed all those puppies."

The boys looked at one another, their excitement building at the miller's long-winded disclosure.

"Well, what did you have in mind?" asked Shikwe at length,

unable to stand the suspense. "What is it with the dogs?"

"The deal, my two friends, is this," said the miller, stubbing out the spent cigarette butt and grinding it in under his heel. "I was thinking of selling a number of the puppies off."

"Is it?" said Shikwe, evidently disappointed. He had half-hoped that Sudi would invite them over to his compound to pick one for free. Shikwe had been desperate for a herding dog to accompany the boys to the grazing fields.

"Indeed," said the miller, opening the sliding barrier that allowed Shikwe's maize to trickle into the mill. "I have been thinking of selling the puppies, but I am willing to give one away, in return for a favor."

The boys watched the miller's face keenly, their hearts beating with excited anticipation. "And what favor would that be, Sudi?" asked Shikwe eagerly.

"You really want the dog, don't you?" asked the miller.

"We sure could do with a herding dog," Andati acknowledged. "Maybe we can train the dog to catch squirrels and rabbits—there are so many to be hunted down in the valley."

"And maybe it's just about time you had one," said the miller, pushing the battered metal pail in place with the toe of his *akala*[26] shoe as the flour started trickling out of the spout. "I had my first hunting dog at about your age; a brown little terror called Popi. I never saw a dog that could pick up the spoor of so many rabbits on a single hunt. And Popi always caught anything that he routed. Not a single rabbit could outrun him! It is a pity he died of old age last year, but not before siring the puppies that now run all over my

---

[26] A hardy handmade sandal cut out of an old automobile tyre, popular among the Maasai herdsmen

compound."

"Is it?" said Shikwe, bright-eyed.

"Indeed. He was a fine stud, too, my Popi was," said the miller, reaching into the folds of his well-worn coat for another cigarette.

"So, what is the favor you had in mind?" asked Shikwe, sizing up to the little miller, impatient with the round-about manner in which everything was unfolding.

"Well, it might even be a puppy for *each* of you, if you do the job well," said the miller, turning the lever that switched off the idling mill.

Shikwe and Andati were silent most of the way back home, each mulling over the miller's strange request.

"Just what do you think they want to do with Uncle Mukolwe?" asked Andati as they neared their compound.

"I've no idea. Maybe they want to teach him a lesson. Give him a beating, perhaps, just to keep him from messing around with other people."

"It could be. If you ask me, I think the man deserves a lesson or two. I hate the way he bosses everyone around. Remember how he slapped us last time he came visiting?"

"How could I forget?" Shikwe replied. "My cheek stung the rest of the day at school. Father doesn't beat us that way, and I do not know why he tolerates Uncle's bullying of us."

"Father cannot stand up to Uncle Mukolwe because Uncle was the one who placed Father in his clerk's job at the sugar factory."

"It figures. Uncle Mukolwe looks to me like a crafty weasel who will offer you a seemingly harmless gift, but later uses the fact that he helped you to visit terror on you every day of your life. Maybe Sudi was telling the truth. And surely Father, too, must be fed up with the man's endless visits and his demands for more money to bail him out all the time."

"So, should we do it?" asked Andati.

"What do you think?"

"I don't know," said Andati with a shrug. "All I know is that I sure could do with a puppy."

"Me too," said Shikwe. "Wow! What fun we'd have with the boys down at the valley!"

"Well, why don't we sleep on it and decide tomorrow?"

"That sounds like a good idea. Nonetheless I can't help but wonder what Uncle Mukolwe did to anger Father, and how the miller is connected to all this. Do you think it is Father's plan to keep Uncle from visiting us anymore?"

"Could be," said Andati with a shrug.

When Uncle Mukolwe alighted from the battered bus at Ekero market the following evening, a number of people stopped to look at him surreptitiously. Uncle Mukolwe, oblivious of the interested glances of the villagers, walked quickly down the street, carrying his worn leather traveling case, his coat draped over one arm, and a well-thumbed newspaper tucked beneath his arm. He paused at a shop to buy some groceries, gifts for those he was visiting, and as he waited for the shopkeeper to wrap up his purchases, Mukolwe removed his shiny leather hat and wiped at his bald head with a crisp white handkerchief.

Among the people keeping a close watch on Mukolwe

were five men seated on the veranda of a little pub directly opposite the bus stop—Andati's father, Sudi, and three others. These silent observers were hidden from view of the road by a screen of bamboo, erected by the proprietor to shield his customers from passersby looking to cadge a drink, as was the custom in this part of the country. The five had just completed a business meeting and were having a beer as they watched, with particular interest, as the traveler removed his hat to wipe at his head.

Down the road, the new mill towered above the rickety shops that made up the market, its new blue roof and white stucco walls gleaming amid the twisted, rusty *mabati*[27] roofs and weathered moss-covered brick. The mill was easily the tallest building, with an upper story that provided storage space for grain. The old delivery truck was parked outside the mill, backed up next to the double steel doors, beside which the night watchman, who had just reported for duty, had settled into his leaning wickerwork chair.

As the traveler collected his purchases and made his way through the narrow passage between the shops, the five men at the pub followed him with their eyes. But they were not the only ones watching.

In a corner of the darkening pub, an old man from the village by the name of Wekulo sat nursing a drink. He was working his way toward spending the last of the lump-sum payment he had received from the sugar company for the delivery of his crop. The barmaids did not pay him much mind—he rarely gave away free drinks and had little interest in idle chatter. The few friends Wekulo still possessed were

---

[27] Corrugated-iron sheet roofing

fewer in number than the fingers of one hand.

Wekulo's pleasure lay in the daily portion of a kilo of roast ribs that the butcher next-door reserved for him, and through which he carved his way with a ritual concentration, using the long pocketknife he carried in his coat pocket. Thereafter, he burped over his beer and picked at his browned teeth with a matchstick as he watched the light slowly fade over the little market. From his vantage point, Wekulo could see everything that went on in the little pub. Indeed, he had been watching the five men at the veranda for the better part of the afternoon.

The old man was not fooled, and neither were the other elderly men of the village. Makokha, the cobbler, had visited his in-laws in Funyula to attend to some urgent business that had arisen; Nangabo, the schoolteacher, had received a summons from the Teachers' Service Commission in Nairobi; and there were others. Mysterious disappearances, all of them, and only one thing in common—the men had all been bald. It was an old story. A bald head was just what the mill needed, if the talisman that had been planted was to work. It had always been that way, whether it was a matter of building roads, cathedrals, factories, or any other construction projects. The machines had to be appeased before they could commence work. It was their way, and had been so ever since the days of their forefathers.

Poor man; walking right into the jaws of a carefully laid snare, the old man thought to himself as he cast a glance at the five men huddled in conspiratorial silence on the veranda.

Shikwe heard the light tapping on the window first. Stiffening, he turned over slowly on the mat and whispered, "*An-dati! Andati!*"

"Oh, I heard it," the other boy whispered back. Although it was pitch dark in the hut, both of them had been wide awake, lying on their backs side by side, waiting for the signal. It had been impossible to go to sleep with the impending business yet to be completed.

Sitting upright, Andati called, "Uncle! Uncle! I need to use the latrine."

The boys listened for a response, but heard only the muffled snore of their uncle and the creak of his bed as he shifted in his sleep. Andati called out again, a little louder, and the two boys listened anxiously for a response, but there was none; none but the deep and steady rhythm of their uncle's wheezy breathing. Moving like phantoms in the dark, the two boys rose slowly to their feet and inched toward the bed.

"Here," Shikwe whispered, pushing a napkin into Andati's hand. Shikwe's voice had a tremor and his hand was trembling. But Andati fared no better for nervousness. They approached their uncle's bed, which had been pushed up against the wall. A shaft of moonlight from the window fell across the bed, partly illuminating the face of the sleeping man. Andati dug into the pocket of his shorts, searching amongst the bric-a-brac he carried there. He found and retrieved the little vial Sudi had given him. Using the light of the moonbeam, Shikwe folded the napkin carefully into a quarter, both their hearts pounding and their breath whistling in their throats in the hushed stillness that had settled over the room.

Andati carefully removed the vial's rubber stopper and poured the liquid over the napkin. "Now!" he whispered

63

softly, nudging Shikwe in the ribs. Shikwe hesitated, and Andati poked him sharply in the ribs with his bony elbow. As Shikwe stepped reluctantly forward, the two boys were startled by a soft rap on the window, and the urgent whisper of the miller.

"Everything ready in there? Hurry up and open the door!" Sudi whispered.

"Come on," whispered Andati earnestly.

Shikwe bent forward and pressed the napkin firmly against his uncle's mouth, squeezing his own eyes tightly shut. Andati added his hand to Shikwe's and both boys held the napkin in place, their limbs seized with nervous trembling.

Only five seconds were needed, Sudi had said. But each passing moment seemed like an eternity. The sweat poured from the boys' brows, their breathing increasingly labored, their eyeballs glowing like white marbles in the dark. Sudi's impatient tapping at the window only added to the boys' growing tension. The sleeping man's breath held in his chest and he snorted deep inside his throat as if he was going to cough. He made the terrifying choking sound again as his breath, failing to exhale, choked him. In the electrified silence it took every ounce of willpower the boys possessed for them to keep the napkin pressed in place. Five seconds seemed an eternity.

Just when the boys were going to loosen their hold on the sleeping man's face and bolt he turned suddenly, his eyes flying open, his head whipping from one side to the other. Marshaling the breath in his tightening chest, Uncle Mukolwe bunched his massive shoulders and flung his arms in a violent motion that threw the boys halfway across the room.

"*Aaaaaghh*!" he gasped, springing upright, his deep baritone startling in the stillness of the night. "*Shetani!*[28] What a demon of a dream!" He swung his legs over the side of the creaky bed, gasping loudly as he groped about in the dark. "Will someone turn on the lamp? Eh? Boys…!"

---

[28] Swahili for "Satan"

CHINESE CUISINE

Fanta sat at the counter of her aunt's shop and watched the street. It was a stifling hot afternoon, and not many people were moving about. She watched the street boy they called Pinchez approach, carrying his grubby, oily sack, a bottle of glue stuck to his upper lip like a ludicrously large boil growing on his mouth.

As soon as Pinchez appeared the street mongrels, which had crawled under the vegetable stalls to escape the heat, sprang up, arranging themselves on either side of the street, their hackles raised, growling deep in their throats. The lad competed with the stray mutts for garbage and food scraps that were tossed into streets.

Fanta wondered that the mongrels did not greet anyone else that way, not even Sudi, the madman, who was equally ragged in appearance. The only other person she knew who provoked such a response was Jomo, who would aggravate the mongrels whenever he set up his *mutura* [29] brazier in the evenings.

Pinchez strolled down the street, his greasy gunny sack swinging across his back, seemingly oblivious of the noisy yaps of the dogs. One of the mongrels lunged at his heel, but Pinchez, watching the pack from the corner of his eye, took a swing at the mutt with his oversize boot. The mon-

---

[29] A long sausage, made of cow or goat intestines, stuffed with minced meat, blood, and chopped onions, and barbecued over a coal-fire

grel, yelping in pain, retreated as the others made energetic but half-hearted lunges at Pinchez's heels.

Pinchez, stopping in front of the shop, leaned back on his stick, gazing at Fanta. At first she pretended not to notice, busying herself arranging and rearranging groceries on the counter. Pinchez liked that. He was watching the way her red print cotton dress hugged her slim back and dipped above her small round buttocks. For the umpteenth time he caught himself wondering why anyone would choose to name their child after a soda. Whatever was her mother thinking to call her Fanta? Perhaps the mother had just downed a soda before she went into labor, Pinchez concluded with amusement. About him, the mongrels had settled back upon their haunches, growling low in their throats, tails stretched straight in the dust, their eyes fixed on him.

Pinchez extracted the glue bottle from where it was wedged under his nose and examined it. He gave the viscous goo at the bottom of the bottle a hard tap against the heel of his hand before returning it to its place under his nostrils. He took a long sensuous pull, the fumes zinging home deep into his nasal cavity and warming the base of his belly. Fanta turned and saw him still standing there, a stupefied grin creasing the cheeks of his grime-coated face. When their eyes met, he winked. She made a face and went back to rearranging the groceries. He liked that very much. The dogs had lost interest in their game and now sprawled on their bellies in the dust, eyeing him and his long stick from a distance.

Leaning on his stick in the dusty street, Pinchez followed Fanta's movements, taking in her thin, pale arms and her translucent albino skin. Her limbs were baby-like, almost like a *mzungu's*,[30] the fine hairs that adorned them like those of a plucked chicken. He didn't care for her rashes, or her pale, pale eyes. But he felt that he could live with those minor imperfections. He wondered what it would feel like to have her arms roped about his neck, how it would feel to have her. Maybe it would be like having a *mzungu*. He had never been with a *mzungu*, but he imagined that she would feel smooth against his skin like…like what? Like an eel. Yes, supple as Fanta might appear, of one thing he was certain—Fanta's body would not be warm next to his.

Pinchez looked up and caught her staring, too. The moment their eyes met, she made a face and turned her back on him, ducking behind the screen that concealed a door to an inner room. Pinchez clicked softly and licked his lips before collecting his gunnysack and setting off down the street. Instantly the dogs sprang up and escorted the boy along his way with their frenzied barking.

As Pinchez scavenged the garbage heaps on the side of the street his mind was whirring. He had been so engrossed in his fantasies he had momentarily forgotten some important business. Kassim, the *mganga*[31] at the bus terminal—who many believed was from Tanzania while he was actually a Wanga from Mumias—had revealed an interesting tidbit the week before. Kassim had sworn him to secrecy then revealed that across the border, in Tanzania, there was a significant demand for albinos like Fanta. The Tanzania *waganga* were doing a booming business, selling amulets prepared using albino body parts. An albino arm, he exclaimed excitedly,

---

[30] Swahili for "white person"
[31] shaman/sorcerer

fetched as much as a quarter of a million shillings.

Now *that* was some money to kill your own mother for! A quarter of a million for just an arm? He wondered if Kassim was fabricating stories as they passed the time sharing a *spliff*[32] in the junk-strewn yard behind his tiny tin-walled shop. But the old man had had a certain look in his eyes, a fervent intensity that convinced Pinchez he had been telling the truth. Kassim had contacts, and if they could only get her across the border....

Pinchez thought about this as he flattened a rusty biscuit tin underneath his oversize Caterpillar boot, a different make and color from the one on his other foot. He opened the gunnysack, and the dogs, which prowled watchfully about his heels, followed his hands as he stuffed the flattened tin within. Wiping his moist brow with the back of one hand, Pinchez raised the sack to his shoulder. As he made his way up the street, his unwelcome entourage in tow, a slow, smug smile spread across his grease-streaked face.

Pinchez knew exactly what needed to be done. First, he would devise a way to lure Fanta into a trap. Then, he would indulge his fantasies...after all, he would have all the time in the world. Thereafter, he would remove his hacksaw, and the rest would be easy, just like sawing through a dog's carcass. Yes, it would be easy, he convinced himself, his breath rasping in his throat with excitement. And he knew just who would lend him a hand—Jomo. That old boy would get into any job for a cut of the takings. Pinchez could already see the glow of excitement in Jomo's eyes at the prospect of such a landfall. It would be up to Kassim to arrange the transport,

---

[32] weed

with half payment due on delivery and the rest when the cargo was handed over at Namanga on the border. Afterwards everyone would get their share, and everyone would be happy.

Pinchez, knowing the wily nature of his potential partners, fully expected that one of them might double-cross him, seeking all the profit for himself. Jomo would insist upon being the boss, right up to when they handed over the cargo, carved up and nicely packed in crates (complete with ice-packs if the blighters who would be paying insisted). But Jomo was unlikely to betray him. Kassim, too, surely knew better than to play around with Pinchez? The old *mganga* would be toying with a razor across the throat, and he knew it. The whole thing was tight as a virgin, Pinchez thought with a laugh.

Pinchez, strolling down the street, broke into a soft whistle as the dogs at his heels launched into an excited frenzy of barking, lopping after him like chase hounds on a hunt.

The rays of the late afternoon sun cast long shadows across the street and lit the rusted, twisted *mabati* shop roofs to a fiery hue that made them look almost beautiful. Shop lights were switching on, one after the other, and music blared from the pub windows. Jomo had set up his *jiko*,[33] but he had yet to turn on his lights. The street mongrels gathered around the greasy spot where the *jiko* stood, in anticipation of castoffs once the evening's business had begun. Jomo arranged the charcoal on the tray and stuffed used packets of

---

[33] coal brazier

milk in the chamber beneath. Then he stood, watching the throngs of people streaming down the street after work, a Rooster cigarette dangling from his mouth, his eyes squinting thoughtfully.

It was mid-month and the street people would have received their advance pay from the Asian factories and the *Wazungu* homes where they worked. The workers would start at the smoky *busaa* shebeens, Jomo knew, and then as the evening ripened, they would stagger to the pub for a beer and a dance with the cunning *busaa*[34] women that hung on their arms. As they filed into the pub the glistening *mutura* and fragrance of roasting meat would be irresistible. By that time of night, a five-shilling measure of the stuffed colon-sausage would cost double. For those who were ashamed of being seen eating *mutura,* Jomo had a lad doing the rounds in the bar, carrying a tray laden with beef samosas. The samosas were irresistible, perfectly spiced with fried onions and chilies, and going for twice the price as the night progressed. With predictable patrons such as these, who needs a miserly job at a *Mhindi's*[35] factory? Living off the fat of the land—wasn't that what the poet called it?

Blowing a long jet of smoke, Jomo shouted at a group of kids playing with a broken tricycle. His son, Gitau, detached himself from the group and came running. Save for his size, the boy was the spitting image of his father, bearing the same broad accountant's forehead and shifty eyes.

---

[34] homemade traditional grain beer
[35] Swahili for an 'Indian.' Asian industrialists dominate in the manufacturing sector in Kenya; but often they pay very poor wages. Lately the Chinese have been making a strong and steady foray into this market.

"I want to find this *jiko* lit up by the time I get back," Jomo instructed his son curtly, before gathering his sack and setting off to get the meat.

Fanta's aunt was a burly, dark woman whose chubby face was perpetually breaking into a smile. This inclination to happiness was the primary reason that she had worked for the white family in the wealthy suburb next to the slum for so many years. She always made their guests feel at ease, her mere presence radiating a friendly warmth in the large airy house. But behind those shiny dark eyes was a sharp business mind that had enabled her to send her three children to good boarding schools upcountry; she was planning to enroll Fanta, with the profits from the grocery store, in a hairdressing course. With this objective in mind, Fanta's aunt took stock at the store every evening.

She wasn't looking very pleased today. The refrigerator remained full of soda, and the shelves of groceries were still well-stocked. Yet it was mid-month, she knew, a time when residents would be replenishing their rice, sugar, and beans or buying a tub of Blue Band with their advance pay.

"I daresay we had a bad day," she said to Fanta, who was sweeping out the yard at the front of the shop. "We have hardly sold a packet of milk!" She turned on the light at the front of the shop, instantly drawing a swarm of mosquitoes and moths, which swirled round and round the glowing bulb. "Finish up the cleaning and come lend a hand," she called to Fanta as the first of the evening customers started lining up at the counter, drawn by her familiar high-pitched voice. Their visitors were mostly women, coming in for a bit of the day's gossip before they purchased a matchbox or a measure of ghee.

Fanta swept the trash into a dustpan and emptied it into the bin on one side of the yard. Seeing the bin was almost full, she decided to empty it on the rubbish heap in the garden behind the store. The garden was weedy, and the sticky blackjack pods attached themselves to the hem of her dress as she passed along the narrow path toward the garbage heap. The stalks of *sukuma wiki* were starting to wither, shoulder-high and stripped of all their leaves. The tomato vines, too, sagged from their stakes like strips of thong, with a few desiccated fruit hanging limply from their weedy branches. When the rains came, Fanta would dig them up in preparation for a new crop.

As Fanta wound her way through the weeds toward the garbage heap, she was thinking of the street mongrels. They had set about barking again, and there was a strange note in the wailing bark that disturbed her. The dogs had retreated to some distance from the shops, their barking echoing across the muddy river that snaked its way down the valley, separating their slum from the one nearby. Fanta recognized that wailing bark—it was the sound of canine terror, a sound the pack usually made in the dead of night when they were cowed and afraid. She knew it well because she had always been a light sleeper.

The sky had grown dark, and Fanta felt a chill pass down her spine. Dusk filled her with dread, an old fear that she had lived with secretly all her life. Fanta had graphic dreams, terrifying dreams, and she would often wake in the night, damp with a cold sweat and a pounding heart. As she stood in the weedy garden—with the faint light of the naked security bulbs playing on the swaying treetops, the fireflies zapping about her, and the forgotten garbage bin clutched in her hands—a cold finger of dread clawed suddenly at her guts.

The cool of the evening chill stirred the fine hairs at the back of her neck, and her ears filled with the eerie wailing of the dogs. The previous night, she had dreamed of the woman fishmonger down the street. The fishmonger had been gutting and cleaning the fish in her old reed basket. She washed the gutted fish in the rusty tin trough, her thick hands moving with the practiced deftness of a reliable old machine. Smoke billowed from her wood-fire, the flames lapping around the sooty pan. The deep-frying oil, leftover from the day before, bubbled angrily around three fish in the pan. A swarm of blue flies hung around the slop bucket, dispersed occasionally by the flywhisk the fishmonger waved in their direction. She rose from her low kitchen stool to turn the frying fish. As she dipped her slice into the frothy oil, the big fish rose upright, suddenly ballooning out as if inflated by an invisible suction pump. In the blink of an eye, the fish had flipped itself over and out of the pan, and towered above the fishmonger, who stood below, aghast. The fish's glassy eyes peered down at the fishmonger, its mouth mockingly curved, and its glistening body bearing the parallel gashes of the fishmonger's knife as she had prepared it for salting.

"Ha! Surprised, aren't we?" the fish said, leaning down toward the dumbstruck woman.

One by one the other fish rose from the pan, arranging themselves around the dumbstruck fishmonger, their eyes coldly menacing, bodies slashed by injuries inflicted by the fishmonger's blade. The woman looked about her for help, but the street had suddenly emptied, and the mangy dogs that slept in the dust seemed entirely uninterested in her predicament.

"Well, looks like a miracle just happened here," the mother fish declared, her full pink lips curling sardonically, her algae-scented breath warm on the face of the witless fishmonger. "Isn't that so, my good lady?" The fishmonger, shocked into silence, had nothing to say. Her mouth opened and closed without a sound escaping.

"I see. So the miracle has robbed you of your voice?" the mother fish said, gesturing at the other fish with a flap of her fin. "In that case, we had better get on with the business at hand. We don't have much time, you see."

A shriek rose at the back of the fishmonger's throat as the fish closed in, but it escaped her constricted throat only as a whimper. The collective fish fins extended outward, encircling her like an octopus's arms, and lifting her off her feet as if she were a piece of sponge.

Lying on the chopping board, the fishmonger vigorously attempted to free herself, but she was held fast by coarse claw-like fins. With the fishmonger thus subdued, the mother fish took charge, seizing the sharp gutting knife that the woman herself had wielded so effectively. The mother fish held the blade up to the flame, scrutinizing the cutting edge, which had been honed to razor sharpness by the knife-grinder earlier that afternoon. A satisfied chortle sounded deep in the fish's throat as she sucked in her bulbous belly and bent over.

The fish first went to work on the fishmonger's broad back, slicing across the quivering spine from shoulders downward. Next, like a seasoned surgeon, creating shallow, neatly parallel gashes, the fish worked the chunky buttocks and flabby thighs, seeming to enjoy the way the blade sank into the soft flesh. The fishmonger shrieked and screamed, jerking violently as salt was poured into the wounds, trying desperately to free herself.

"Some spice perhaps?" asked the mother fish, gazing round at her mates. One of the fish proffered a tub of ground pepper, the kind the fishmonger used to extend the shelf-life of the little fish as they awaited their customers. The mother fish worked up a thick paste that would cover the fishmonger's body and went to work, kneading the pepper thoroughly into the flesh until her captive was red as a beetroot from head to toe. Then she stood back, a satisfied smile spreading on her face.

"Now for the mouth-watering part," she said softly, indicating the pan that was still boiling angrily above the raging flames. As the fishmonger was being lowered headfirst into the frothing brown oil, Fanta awoke, gasping for air in the thick darkness, her body drenched in sweat.

Jomo watched as Pinchez lowered the greasy gunny sack from his shoulder and rummaged inside, pulling out the carcass. They were hidden deep in the thickets, the sluggish river gurgling behind them, the mosquitoes rising like a swarm of angrily buzzing bees from the *nduma*[36] marsh. The stench of urine and human excrement kept visitors away, and made

---

[36] arrowroot

the thickets a convenient place to conduct business. They glanced down the path, hemmed in by post and rails and a string of shaggy kei apple hedges, toward where it looped behind the last row of shanties. The bridge was deserted and they could hear snatches of the seven o'clock news from a tinny black-and-white TV through the window of a tin-walled shanty. Secure in the knowledge that they would not be interrupted, Jomo and Pinchez returned their attention to the still-warm carcass. It was barely a few minutes dead, with the blood clotting over the ugly wound on the head where Pinchez had bashed it in with a brick.

But what surprised Jomo was not the carcass, but the co-lour of the fur.

"This is the big one that sits outside the bar with the *askari*[37] at night, isn't it, Pinchez?" Jomo asked in a whisper, peering closely at the white patch on the animal's neck and the claws on the forelegs that had been well exercised on the arms of the *askari*'s old armchair until the fake leather had been rent to strips and its cotton stuffing spilled.

"You said you wanted a fat one for mid-month, didn't you?" Pinchez challenged.

"Well—"

"Well, what?" Pinchez demanded, holding the carcass high for Jomo's examination. "It is just what you said… look at the flanks. I daresay we are talking about twenty or so kilos here."

"It's just that…well, I didn't—"

"Look, Jomo," Pinchez said irritably, straightening up, a gleaming carving knife appearing suddenly in his hand. "Cut

---

[37] guard

out that well…well…business. Don't tell me now that I went to all this trouble for nothing." His eyes flashed in the fading light.

"Oh, relax, Pinchez, I didn't mean that," said Jomo, patting him on the shoulder. "Put it down. Let's get to work before it is dark. It's just that…I didn't expect you to raid the very place where we do business. The old barman was rather fond of the old bitch, you know—bringing it bones and all that."

'Well, I suppose he'll just have to find himself another bitch," said Pinchez, with a hoot of laughter. Jomo cackled appreciatively, clapping his co-conspirator on the shoulder. "Business is business, Jomo, you know," said Pinchez as their laughter died down. "I guess you never wondered why the rest of the pack was barking like mad monkeys, did you?"

"I should have guessed. All the same, you are one hell of a devil, Pinchez."

Pinchez bared his last tooth in a hideous grin, squatting over the spread-eagled carcass. "Well, you will have to upgrade that to Lucifer himself after you hear what plan Kassim and I have in mind. It will make this business at hand seem like nursery school."

The two men worked together in silence, their hands moving in deft synchronicity as they flayed the skin off the carcass. They had worked together on a number of carcasses; once, Pinchez found a massive snake on the highway that had been partially flattened under a truck's tire.

"Chinese cuisine, that's what your customers will have today. They say it tastes just like fish," Pinchez had said, flashing his one-toothed grin as he unceremoniously chopped off the snake's head. "Further still, I hear fine belts are made out of snake hide."

On another occasion, they had plucked a marabou stork, a huge mountain of a bird with a bulging mouth sack beneath its bill. They had argued over whether to include the flapping sack in the meat pot or whether they should discard it.

After the carcass had been skinned, Jomo examined the animal's head.

"What are you thinking, Jomo?" Pinchez asked, his bloodied hands dangling over his bony knees.

"You could have found another way to take the old bitch," he muttered. "You know how much money a goat's head brings in?"

Pinchez laughed, scoffing. "You would need nothing short of magic to sell that," he said, poking the bloodied head, "even to a blacked-out barfly."

"I can make four litres of *muteta*[38] soup out of this head," Jomo replied, musingly. "That way it doesn't have to appear on the table."

"Now you are thinking like a genius!" Pinchez exclaimed. "You never leave anything for the vultures, do you, Jomo?"

"Why should I feed them? What work have they ever done for me?"

"You know, one day we are going to make enough money from this business and retire," Pinchez remarked, rummaging in his sack for his rusty hacksaw. "Yes, it will happen someday. With our two brilliant minds working together we'll

---

[38] Traditional soup made out of a boiled goat's head and garnished with bitter-tasting herbs that are believed to counter gout, low libido, and weight gain in men who drink plenty of beer. The herbs are sourced from Maasai herbalists. This soup is very popular with older Kikuyu men in Central Kenya.

haul in enough to buy a bus, perhaps—or a couple of taxis."

"You are starting to drift off," said Jomo. "I have never believed in fluffy dreams."

"You think so? The money we could make in this deal of Kassim's would set us up to retire. What do you say, Jomo? Is that really dreaming?"

"Look, let's get this job done first. The customers are not going to wait forever, you know."

"You are right."

As they opened the belly cavity to release the steamy offal, Pinchez froze, his head cocked. He had developed, over the years, a powerful sense for detecting when something was amiss, and at that moment, his skin prickled and the fine hairs at the back of his neck stood up.

"Jo—" he began, but the words died on his lips when he lifted his head. The afternoon clouds had cleared, and in the pale light of the emergent moon the bushes had parted to reveal the silhouette of a third presence. Indeed, it seemed that she had been standing there for some time, watching.

In the moonlight, her skin was even paler, her shoulders frail and delicate, her slender arms and legs scratched from bush thorns. Her eyes were alert, but she appeared rooted in place, frozen like a marble statue that had materialized inexplicably out of the dark. The pale, chapped lips of her mouth hung open, slack.

Pinchez stood first, reaching for a weapon in the sack beside him. Jomo began to rise from his squat. Fanta knew him well—her cousins often bought *mutura* from him when they came home for the holidays. As the men moved deliberately toward her, she suddenly understood the danger. Their gazes

80

had shifted, from a startled surprise to a dark deliberation. Fanta, electrified into motion, knew instinctively that her life was threatened.

At that instant, the shop's back door was flung open, and in the rectangle of light, her aunt's burly figure appeared.

"Fanta! You hard-of-hearing girl, where are you? Fanta...!"

In the ensuing months Fanta's relations agonized over what had happened to her. The girl had not only gone dumb, but would no longer sleep alone. She became hysterical at the prospect, and would cling desperately to her aunt, her breath strained in her throat, her eyes wide with fright, her body trembling like a child's. She stayed indoors and refused to remain alone at the shop. Neither would she be sent on an errand. She would watch the street from behind the shop counter with scared eyes. Her cousins tried to cajole her back into her old complacency; her aunt prepared her favorite food, but it was all in vain. In the end, Fanta's family decided to send her back upcountry, hoping the fresh country air would do her good. And it did. A few days after she arrived, she uttered her first word in four months: "Killers."

TOMMY HILFIGER

Jamin and Alice were in a scare. The boss was not in a good mood, and from the thumping coming from upstairs as he rummaged through furniture, fuming like a caged bush elephant, it was not a small matter that would end in the bedroom. Alice added more washing fluid to the sink and worked up a bubble of suds. Then she dipped her hands in the warm water and went back to cleaning the greasy plates, scrubbing furiously with the sponge. Through the window she could see Jamin equally busy scouring the tires of the car, reaching underneath the front fender to scrape away the brown Mara mud before putting the hose to it. Just like Alice he was trying to ignore the tirade coming from upstairs even though he expected the kitchen door to come crashing open any time and his boss to come barging out, his rotund face red as a tomato, baying for someone's blood. Over at the guard's hut, Odipo, the day guard, switched off his portable radio and stood at attention by the gate, pretending to scrutinize passersby, but all the while straining to catch a word of the tirade upstairs.

What could the matter be? they all wondered. Could it be one of those bedroom arguments? It seemed highly unlikely. The two of them were like two loving doves in a nest. How many times had they spontaneously given Jamin and Alice a day off so that they could be alone in the house? On days like this, the madam would often bring Odipo his flask of tea unusually early; his tea might be accompanied by sandwiches carefully packed in an ice cream tub, or left-overs from their own meal the evening before—usually *biriani*[39] from a take-away restaurant, in which would be tucked a chicken wing or a half-gnawed drumstick. And from the way she locked the front door Odipo knew that their business for the day was ended.

Later Odipo would espy them, through gaps in the curtains, walking naked in the house, sometimes dancing to soft music from the stereo, or Madam clapping her hands and dancing as Harrison strummed his guitar and sang a country song. Thereafter, they would swim and then lounge on the chaise longues by the poolside, Madam drinking a cocktail and Harrison a whisky, both of them still in their birthday suits. Later in the evening they would light a bonfire on the back lawn and grill lamb chops or chicken wings, which they washed down with wine by candlelight because the security lights on that side of the compound would not have been turned on.

Odipo knew all this because he had been working for them for eight years. He knew too that Harrison liked to make love on the balcony of their upstairs bedroom on a moonlit night, while Madam liked to do it on the rug by the log fire in the living room. This he had gleaned from Ali, the night guard, who equally made it his business to know everything that went on in the home that he guarded. They knew that Harrison was a fine stud who knew his job well—if madam's screams during the marathon sessions were anything to go by. And so, what could the fuss in the bedroom be all about?

---

[39] spicy Indian rice

Alice lifted her eyes from the dishes and glared at Jamin through the open kitchen window. Jamin winked at her and made a lewd sign with his hand over his crotch, leaning over the water-slicked bonnet of the car and humping it like a horny bull on a heifer. Alice made a face and wagged a finger at him, causing Jamin's face to split in a grin, baring a mouthful of irregular teeth stained grey from numerous visits to the *busaa* dens in the neighboring shanty town. Odipo caught sight of Jamin's antics and turned his face away, stifling a laugh. He was in the direct view from the master bedroom and he knew that Harrison or Madam could see him if they chanced to look out the bay window.

Soon Harrison's heavy footsteps were heard coming down the stairs, the wood creaking beneath his mammoth weight. "Alice!" he called in his bawling voice, one that Madam said he had inherited from his deep-sea fishermen ancestors who had been famous whalers in the Antarctic. "A-a-a-lice!"

"Yes, boss," said Alice, dumping the plate she was washing in the sink and hurrying to the foot of the stairs, drying her hands on her gingham apron.

"I cannot find my new set of underwear. Did you wash them for me when you last did the laundry?" Even this early in the morning his round face was flushed red, his breath huffing out of his massive chest as if from some heavy exertion.

"You mean the white ones, boss?" asked Alice, her hands wringing nervously.

"Yes. The Tommy Hilfigers I brought with me from safari last week. There is only one pair left. And yet I bought seven of them, one for each day of the week."

"But I washed all of them last Saturday, boss," said Alice earnestly. "I remember hanging them out on the line in the backyard to dry like you instructed, boss." Her lips were quivering, a layer of moisture glistening on her brow at the prospect of losing her job. Finding a job in Nairobi these days was like searching for a tree frog in the Sahara. "I swear I left them on the line when I left at midday."

"Well, like I said, I can't find them. They are not here. Today is Friday, and there's supposed to be a last pair. It is not there!"

"But, boss…" Alice's lips quivered uncontrollably as she searched for words to explain. But before she could say anything he swept past her with a dismissive wave of the hand, banging against the bank of washing machines lined up against the wall and out the door, his ham fists swinging furiously.

"Jamin! Ja-a-a-min!"

"Yes, boss," said Jamin, dropping the wet cloth in the soapy bucket and hurrying over, drying his hands on the seat of his green khaki overalls.

"Who took my underwear from the clothesline?" said Harrison, towering over the diminutive gardener.

"Your what, sir…?" said Jamin, his eyes wide, hands trembling by his sides.

"My *underwear*, didn't you hear me? My new white Tommy Hilfigers. Did you take them?"

"I…I…I've never seen them, sir," said Jamin in a stammer, his lips quivering, head shaking vehemently.

"Oh, so you mean a ghost came out of nowhere and disappeared with them, is that what you are saying? Huh? You mean they disappeared by themselves…?"

But before Jamin could answer he stomped off.

"Odipo! O-o-odiiipooo!"

"Yes, boss," said Odipo, hurrying over on the double, his heels clicking on the tarmac.

"My underwear…who took my new Tommy Hilfigers?"

"I…I…" Odipo was trembling so much the words just wouldn't come. His wife had just given birth the week before and the last thing he wanted to think of was the possibility of being laid off work. "I…I swear, boss, I do not know," he stammered, dropping to his knees, hands raised in supplication.

"Wha…who…?" For a while Harrison's huge red jowls worked like a bulldog's, saliva spraying from his lips, eyes flashing like those of a wounded hammerhead shark. Then his heavy hands flopped to his sides and he stormed back toward the house. "Idiots! Bloody thieving idiots!" In his rage, his thick neck had withdrawn even further into his prizefighter's shoulders, his head bobbing back and forth like a Neanderthal's. The doors rattled on their frames as he slammed them behind him, cracking like pistol shots through the corridors of the sprawling villa.

That Saturday, at the dance in the region of the shanty-town known as Congo, Jamin finally won the heart of the chocolate-skinned big-bottomed serving girl, Salima. Late-night revelers drooled every time she bent over to pour them a drink, their besotted minds weaving exotic fantasies about a night enveloped in her supple arms, their heads resting on her full breasts.

It was past midnight when the resident band upped the tempo—the drummer beating his palms into a frenzy on the makeshift drum set, fashioned out of old oil drums. The three-piece homemade guitars shrieked as they strained to follow the undulating lead of the *litungu*[40] player, who bobbed his shiny bald head up and down on his sweat-slicked shoulders, like a blue-headed *obongo-bongo* lizard in an old flame tree, his pink tongue lolling out of his wet mouth as his buttocks waggled on his low stool to the carnal banging of the ring on his big toe against the shiny arm of the lyre. Taking his cue, the soloist soared above the frenetic melodies, his voice quivering in a timbre that caused the hearts of his audience to melt. By this late hour the yard had grown dim, lit only by the glow of the security lights set high on the perimeter fence of the neighboring Braeburn School.

One by one the revelers started to strip. The men tore off their shirts and strutted bare-chested around the circle, teasing the women, who removed their blouses, leaving their brassieres in place as they paired up on the dance floor. But in the heat of the dance the brassieres too would fly off so that the men and women would dance breast to breast. It was the hour of the *tindikiti* love-dance.

Jamin wriggled out of his designer muscle shirt and threw it at the friend he had been sharing a pot with, taking a long drink of the lukewarm *busaa* out of his plastic straw. Then he strutted onto the dance floor, legs bent at the knees, elbows tucked in, hands flopping in the manner of a duck about to take to wing, and slim hips swaying expertly to the beat of the band. As his bottom swung the waistband of his

---

[40] The eight-stringed lyre of the Luhyia tribe of Western Kenya.

distressed jeans sagged lower, riding low upon his hips and piling around his sneakers in the sagging look of the yoyos.[41] Jamin's back pocket bulged with a thick wallet stuffed with payday money, which he carelessly flaunted. Above the hem of his sagging jeans, his bright new boxers glowed in the dim light, just like the heroes of the gangster videos he had seen in number 48 *matatu* shuttle vans. The blue-and-red label on the rucked band of the slightly oversized boxers was stark against his sweaty dark skin, and that succeeded in drawing even more attention to his wiggling hips and his fat wallet.

Jamin saw Salima approach from the corner of his eye. She was carrying a huge frothing pitcher, weaving her way through the crowded dancers to replenish a pot at the far end of the yard. He was watching her keenly, and he saw the way her mascaraed eyes followed the thick wallet stuffed in his back pocket. All the girls in the place, Jamin knew, were openly eyeing him, even as they pretended to listen to the men who had accompanied them. He had selected his clothes most carefully, from the Converse sneakers to the fake gold chain on his wrist, and he knew that he could have just as easily fit in at one of those high-end hang-outs in Westlands where Harrison occasionally took Madam for a drink and dance Saturday evenings. His dance moves had been well rehearsed from a DVD he had bought from a *matatu tout*[42] he knew on the 48 route. It was only his English

---

[41] The showy and fashionable moneyed young men and women of Nairobi's middle class.

[42] A bus conductor, staffing the privately owned public service vans and buses. Usually they compete for customers by hanging out the bus door or window and shouting out their routes and fares. They are often very rude, aggressive, street-wise, and foul-mouthed.

that would give him away in a yoyo crowd. He swung his hip, bumping into Salima as she passed, winking lewdly at her.

"Tonight the *choma*[43] and drinks are all on me," he whispered into her ear. "I'll buy you as much Guinness as you want. What do you say we find a more decent pub to go to, my lovely?"

Salima made a face at him, her deep dark eyes rolling, her thick soft lips forming a seductive pout. But even as she brushed past he knew he had not wasted his words. For when Jamin staggered home to his tiny quarters behind the garage later that night his prize was leaning on his shoulder. He had had to drag Salima out of the taxi, which had halted some distance from the gate to the compound, so as not to attract undue attention. When Ali, the night guard, saw them coming up the dimly lit street, the corners of his lips lifted in a knowing smile. By the time Jamin had bribed Ali sufficiently to allow him to slip Salima into the servants' quarters without waking Harrison, his erstwhile bulging wallet had shrunk alarmingly. But it had been money well spent.

Two weeks later, Jamin had almost forgotten the lovedance, and the way Salima's bare breasts had brushed against his chest. He had a long month ahead and an empty wallet. He was in a perpetually foul mood, and he took to haggling with Alice in an effort to borrow money from their women's *chama*[44] account. Given Jamin's prior refusal to pay interest on

---

[43] Swahili for 'barbecued beef.' A delicacy in Kenya, especially with beer drinkers.

[44] A merry-go-round group (mostly for women) where the members pool their money at the end of every month and give it to one member to invest in a project of their choice; this is repeated monthly until every member has received their pooled kitty, after which the group breaks up or the cycle starts all over again. Sometimes they lend out a

loans of this kind, his inveigling was frequently to no avail. Preoccupied by his lack of funds, Jamin made endless simple mistakes and was often berated by Harrison or Madam.

Harrison and Madam had just returned from another game drive to the Mara for the weekend when Odipo noticed the flat tire on their Range Rover—the perfect opportunity to get a tip from the boss.

Jamin hurried up to the front door and took a deep breath before pressing the buzzer.

"What is it, now?" Harrison barked, his face flushed from the treadmill. "Do you need another loan for your sick brother upcountry, Jamin?" His voice was mocking; he had known Jamin long enough to understand the manner of the man.

"No, boss. It is a flat," Jamin replied, licking his lips nervously. "You have a flat tire."

"Oh, shit," Harrison snapped, drying his moist face on his face towel. "Just when I need to get to an important meeting!"

"I can fix it, boss," said Jamin, eagerly.

"Can you?"

"Sure, boss," said Jamin with a nod. "Odipo can help me with the jack."

"Well, let me find the keys. You'll find all you need in the boot. I hope you know how to do this?"

"Very well, boss. I have done it before," Jamin said, nodding eagerly. From the corner of his eye he caught Odipo watching him from his hut, a grin spreading across his face as Harrison disappeared into the house.

---

portion of the kitty to either the members or outsiders at set interest rate. They can also choose to invest jointly in a major project.

They were just completing the job—Odipo leaning on the wrench one last time to test the firmness of the bolts before Jamin could lower the jack—when Harrison, placing his gator-skin briefcase on the tarmac, kicked the tire with his shiny boot, testing the pressure.

"Well, you seem to have done it well," Harrison said approvingly. He wore a navy Hugo Boss jacket, which creased up under his armpits and hugged his midriff, like a Fiji rugger centre forward dressed up for a Parisian fashion show.

"Thank you, boss," said Jamin with a grin that exposed the last rotten tooth at the back of his mouth.

"Well, take out the jack then. I expect you will be looking forward to a tip, right?"

The grin remained on Jamin's lips as he bent to press the button that deflated the hydraulic jack. Harrison reached for his patent leather wallet, but his hand froze in mid-air. As Jamin had knelt to deflate the jack, the tail of his shirt had pulled upward, exposing his trouser waistband and a portion of his bare back.

"Ja-a-min?" said Harrison in the low drawn-out tone they all dreaded.

Jamin turned slowly, a cold dread creeping up his spine.

"No! Stay right where you are...don't move an inch!" barked Harrison. "Odiipooo! Come here!"

Odipo hurried round the side of the car. Harrison's gaze was fixed on Jamin's exposed back, and the rucked hem of the designer boxer shorts that peeped from beneath the waistband of his old corduroy pants—no longer dazzling white, but the navy and red label unmistakable.

❧

Harrison's face was flushed as he stood over Jamin, who hurriedly threw his possessions into a big yellow SEE-BUY-FLY nylon bag. The enraged *mzungu* herded him through the compound gate, towering over Jamin like a giant as the servant lugged his bag and his hastily rolled mattress on his back.

"Close the gate!" barked Harrison, and Odipo dragged the heavy gates into place, swinging the iron chain through its holes and snapping shut the thick Viro padlock.

For a while the big man paced up and down the drive, his huge arms working restlessly like logs swinging from his shoulders, jaw clenching and unclenching as he ruminated on his terrible anger. Then he lumbered into the house, snatched up the car keys on the little bureau in the hallway and reemerged. Perhaps it was the fact that the little fellow had worked for him for nine years; or perhaps it was that the little bugger's mind worked like a computer during a crisis. Of all Harrison's employees, Jamin was the only one who knew where to get a plumber in the middle of the night when the tank in the ceiling above the study started leaking; he was the only one who could locate a technician whenever the television decoder started acting up, minutes before a crucial Manchester United match. Jamin was a useful bugger, his numerous faults notwithstanding.

Harrison climbed into the car and slammed the door shut. Odipo ran to open the gates as the huge Range Rover roared into life and backed out of the parking bay. With a loud screech that left a layer of rubber on the tarmac, Harrison rocketed out of the compound, missing the gatepost by an inch. He caught up with the weeping Jamin a little distance down the road. As the car screeched to a halt, Jamin jumped into the gutter, the rolled mattress flying out of his grasp, poised to bolt like a cat whose tail was on fire. Harrison leaned over and opened the back door. "Get in!" he shouted.

Jamin gathered his possessions and piled into the car, almost wetting himself with fright. They sped off down the road, a tense silence filling the air between them. It was only when they turned into the gates of the nearby police station that it dawned on Jamin where he was being taken.

The OCS had had dealings with Harrison before. The beefy cop palmed the two thousand shillings the *mzungu* passed under the table, his huge fist disappearing into the pocket of his pants as a huge grin lit up his darkly moist face. Then he rose, bawling at the boys in the other room as he adjusted his belt over a girth that rivaled Harrison's.

"Tell them not to get overzealous. I don't want him hurt," Harrison muttered, rising from the battered visitor's chair.

"Don't worry, *bwana*," the cop replied, smiling. "I know my job."

Then, slapping his visitor on the shoulder, the cop escorted Harrison from the drab office and on his way.

When the Range Rover turned up the following morning, Jamin slid into the rear of the car and cowered in the far corner, whimpering like a beaten puppy. Despite the sting of his rear end and the fresh memory of the bamboo cane descending, Jamin was grateful a hundred times over that he was going back with the boss.

KING OF THE NIGHT

He lay on his back in the dark, listening to the sounds of the night. He could hear the echoing call of a night bird in the trees outside, and the chirps of countless crickets and cicadas that lived in the tall gum and flame trees that surrounded the school compound. If he listened keenly enough he could even catch the gossamer swish of the ghost's long robes as he took his daily night tour. All the boys knew that the founder of the school, the *mzungu*, was buried beneath the massive rock by the toilets; and that at night the rock shifted and his restless ghost came out to torment night stalkers and to choke those sleeping boys who had spoken ill of him while awake. Inside the dormitory the muted snores of his mates resonated from one end of the old hall to the other, some soft and feathery, and others deep and nasal like a sewer toad in a pipe. Intermittent sighs provided the occasional break in this sing-song chorus as someone rolled over.

He shifted slowly to his left, easing the pressure on his right ribs. The thin blanket spread across the bedsprings did little to cushion the curled wires that cut into his back. The school matron had removed his mattress because his term's tuition and boarding fees had not been paid. But it scarcely mattered; he had already made up his mind to escape this dreary ghost-infested place, and he thought longingly of the open spaces of the country and swimming with the village lads in the muddy river down in the valley.

It was a chilly night, but he was fully dressed in his green jersey, khaki shorts, nylon socks, and black leather shoes. He could feel his toes pulse inside the stiff shoes and knew they would be a pale grey come morning, the skin wrinkled and sore. Uncomfortable as his shoes were, he couldn't take them off because come dawn he wanted to get up, slip out of bed, and bound out of the place like a silent and stealthy ninja. There was no need to risk waking the dorm prefect and spoiling the show as he groped for his shoes under the bed.

A hearty fart exploded at the far end of the dorm like a punctured balloon, the exhaust petering out at leisure. A startled cockroach—one of those giant brown ones that lived in the school's sewer system—paused in its exploration of a carton box, its feelers probing the air for a sign of danger. A little distance away a squealing argument arose between two mice fighting over a morsel, their claws scratching the dusty cement. All these vermin that had crawled out of their crevices at lights-out had come close to starving in the four weeks the school had been closed for the holidays. Now was the time to make up for lost calories.

The occupant of the bunk beneath turned over and scratched himself, the scrape of his fingernails raking a buttock amplified in the dead silence, after which he resumed his rhythmic snore.

It amused him to listen to these sounds. He was like a lone sentinel in a graveyard, with only the faceless, formless ghosts for company. He was like God in a morgue of prostrate corpses, with all the time on His hands to select His chosen few. In the still of night, there was no difference between the wealthy students from Nairobi who hauled trunks crammed with expensive crepe-paper-wrapped delicacies purchased in top stores in the city, and the likes of village kids like him, with barely twenty shillings to their name, and who brought fried white ants and roasted groundnuts wrapped in old newspaper as snacks. The night made equals of them all.

For a while he toyed with the idea of getting up and joining the cockroaches and the mice in their feast. He could work the trunks and lockers from one end of the dorm to the other, taking what he wanted. The metal trunks were easily broken into; all he needed to do was lean his weight on the centre of the top and slowly twist one corner upwards, creating space enough for his hand to slip through. Why, he could have buttered bread and marmalade, or chapattis with fried chicken; or even char-grilled fish and chips. The mere thought of these culinary delights caused his belly to turn over in an angry rumble, disturbing the baked mélange of arrowroot and cassava that he had consumed at home earlier that day.

He lay panting softly in the dark, watching the shifting shadows thrown by the security light outside play on the cobwebbed roof. On this first day, the shifting shadows were an alien sight. In his family hut in his village, the night plunged into pitch dark after the tin lamp was doused. As the shadows wove into each other, so did his thoughts swirl, and he thought of a movie they had watched in the assembly hall the previous term. Say, what if he were Count Dracula? Why, he would have a feast, moving from one still body to the next....

He squeezed his eyes shut for a while, and his thoughts shifted to the fat school matron in her crisp starched uniform standing at the head of the dining room stairs, a bunch of store keys dangling from her thick ringed finger. Her chubby face swam in and out of his vision like an image reflected in a rippling pond, her eyes hard like polished black stones. She seemed the very image of a jailhouse keeper, smugly satisfied that not one convict had escaped in the night.

He opened his eyes, a thin smile spreading slowly across his face.

The night dragged on, the light shifting ever so slowly through the gap between the roof and the wall. He remained alert, while everyone else had succumbed to sleep.

He knew just when dawn was approaching and could sense the night wearing itself out. The din of crickets faded slowly as the little fellows tired out. The strange flapping and sighing sounds from the trees ceased as the ghost completed his sojourn and returned to his resting place and the pin-drop silence of the netherworld. There was a brief lull just before dawn, where he could hear the reluctant sigh as night let go its stranglehold. The dew would be at its thickest now in the valley back home, the chill biting to the bone. It was also the hour when the shortwave frequency on his dad's wooden Philips transistor radio would be clearest. There was a sudden clarity to everything at this hour before dawn.

From a distance he heard the first stirrings of the cockerels in the nearby village and the sharp call of the peculiar bird that resided in the tall trees that lined the schoolyard. This harsh bird cry rose above the other birds, slicing through the matted cobwebs of dawn like a hot knife through butter. It wasn't exactly musical, but it was hard to ignore. He had never heard the call outside the school and had yet to discover the identity of the bird that made it. Nevertheless, it seemed as if the bird called to him most particularly, as if bird and boy knew each other intimately, even though they had never met.

It was time to go.

He rose slowly on his elbow, rolling over with hardly a creak of the rusty springs. He swung his legs over the side and lowered himself carefully, supporting himself on his bent elbows until his feet touched the frame of the lower bunk. A warm musky smell that had accumulated through the night hung in the narrow corridor between the rows of bunks. He padded down the aisle, walking carefully on his toes, and pausing by the bunk where Ojamaa, the dorm bully, slept. Despite his intimidating physique, Ojamaa slept naked like a baby, his fat belly bared, his limbs thrown out so that his hands and feet hung over the bedframe. It would have been satisfying, he thought as he paused, to puncture that fat belly and give the bully a taste of the misery he inflicted on everyone else.

The front door's heavy iron bolt eased back with a grating screech, his body tensing with the sudden adrenalin that coursed through his veins. Leaning on the heavy wooden door, he eased it open an inch, the wood scraping faintly on the sandy cement, and slipped out into the cold night.

The dawn chill slapped him in the face, stinging his cheeks. The mist had settled around the naked security bulbs strung high around the square, dimming their light to a hazy glow. He made his way along the whitewashed wall and slipped into the shadows, pausing to survey the silent square, his ears cocked for the slightest sound. From his nighttime vigils he knew that the night guards rarely patrolled the school grounds at this hour. He could hear their boots clamp on the cement walkways only up to just past midnight, then they went away to curl up in their long woolen coats in their sentry boxes. Assured that there was no one about, he turned away and slipped into the night.

The security light at the school gate was dim in the early mist, but he could well imagine the sprawled form of one of the night guards inside his wooden hut that leaned at an angle against the gatepost. The charcoal brazier at the guard's feet had long since burned out, and now he would be curled tightly within his old trench-coat, knees drawn up and chin tucked into his collar for warmth.

The old guard was rumoured to be the lightest sleeper, however, and the last thing he needed was a rusty arrow fired off in alarm sticking into his backside. Cautiously skirting the gate, he scampered deftly on the balls of his feet, feeling like a furtive night-stalking ninja. Coming to an opening in the fence, where the boys usually crawled out to buy home-made cane gin and cheap sex with old hags who smoked filterless cigarettes with the lit end sticking in their mouths at the village, he flopped down on his belly and was out in a flash.

Dusting down the front of his green jersey, he walked briskly past the gate and the slumbering guard, blowing into his palms before digging them deep into his pockets. The road was clear, without a soul in sight. From the main road ahead he could hear the roar of the cane tractors as they hauled their night loads to the factory. The *thump-thump* of the pump at the nearby water pumping station accompanied the whine of the tractors.

Strolling past the village *duka,* he heard a low growl as the bony black dog stirred from its nap on the verandah. Close by, its minder was miles away in dreamland, wrapped up in his long night coat, his guard duty forgotten. He scooped up a handful of pebbles, ready to hurl them at the dog if need be, but the shaggy beast lost interest and went back to sleep.

As he neared the cluster of shops opposite the church he saw someone up and about. It was a man, and he was walking briskly toward him from the side path that passed behind the shops. The boy's heart drummed violently in his chest as he realized the man's identity—the school's duty master who lived in the nearby town. The boy hastened his pace, crossing to the other side of the road, but the faster he walked, the faster the teacher approached, and it became apparent that there was no way the meeting could be avoided. And, indeed, the man's eyes were trained on him.

Just at that moment a cane tractor roared, its headlights stabbing the dawn as it trundled rapidly down the murram road, the bloated trailer swaying from side to side as the huge hind wheels bumped in and out of ruts and potholes. Surprised, and clearly illuminated in the tractor's headlights, the boy saw the duty master raise his arm and prepare to dash across the road.

The tractor rumbled between them, the loose cane protruding from the trailer, and whipping the air dangerously behind, the roar of the exhaust and the crunch of the huge wheels on the murram, drowning out the duty master's words. The boy ran fast alongside the tractor, making for the line of shops. He could hear the duty-master's shoes pounding along the road as he sped after him, shouting at him to stop. At the shops, the boy cut across the road and ducked into a narrow lane. The alley opened into an unkempt yard full of scrub and thorn bush, which served as a dump for the neighboring shopkeepers. The duty-master raced into the overgrown yard and stopped, panting heavily. While the teacher combed the bushes, his ears cocked for the slightest sound, all he saw were the scrawny grey cats that paused in their scavenging, eyeing him malevolently. Cursing, he kicked at a margarine tin and turned, wiping the moisture from the exertion off his brow.

Crouched behind a guava thicket, the boy watched the duty master until he finally departed. He knew that the teacher would, before the hour was out, ring the assembly bell for roll call, after which the boys would go into the mess hall for their breakfast of half-cooked porridge.

He slipped his hand into his pocket to reassure himself that the bus-fare money was still there, then walked toward the bus park. He could see the first of the day-school students hurrying up the road to beat the duty-master's bell. These boys, from the villages surrounding the town, were easy to differentiate from the boarders—their shirts were almost always crinkled from leaf-soap, and near to threadbare from a thorough dashing against the stream-side rocks; the shorts, patched on the seat from wear.

The day-school students possessed the unkempt look of goatherds, their feet cracked from a daily acquaintance with the morning dew and a lifetime's lack of shoes. Unlike the boarders who would have a proper barber clip their hair in stylish cuts and apply brilliantine through it, the coarse kinky hair of the day-scholars was often roughly cut using blunt tailors' shears that left bumpy ridges criss-crossing their scalps like patterned melons. These students carried a distinct smell, which came from their early dip in the river and a thorough scrub of river sand and tallow soap. He knew these things because he, too, was a village boy. As they hurried along in nervous anticipation of another grinding day of tolling bells and freshly cut cypress canes whacking wriggly bottoms, he had no qualms about heading in the opposite direction.

A rickety, patchy, tarp-roofed *matatu* van that leaned heavily on its hind wheels like a sick old dog was waiting at the head of the bus queue, its engine idling to prevent another jump-start. A few passengers were crammed inside the low-slung smoky cab, waiting for it to fill up. He squeezed inside, and as he made himself comfortable on the hard bench that quivered to the rhythm of the spluttering engine, a low sigh of pure joy escaped him. He could already savour the smell of home in his nostrils.

A CALL FROM DOWN UNDER

Demosh was a tough guy, who lived his life in the fast lane. He got what he wanted, and he feared no one. He had money, he had bling, and he could have any girl he wanted in Kangemi. Most important of all, he commanded respect—albeit, a fragile respect born from raw fear.

Demosh sat at the bar at Bottom-line Pub with his lackeys around him, waiting patiently to prove a little man wrong. This diminutive fellow, a stranger to the neighbourhood, had issued a challenge to Demosh and everyone had crowded around the bar, eager to watch the action.

A stack of crumpled old notes—confirmed by the bartender to be five thousand shillings—sat on the bar, next to a glass and three 750-ml bottles of Safari Cane liquor. The stranger perched on his stool at the end of the bar, a curious smile playing about his thin lips, his bloodshot eyes still struggling with yesterday's hangover.

Demosh cleared his throat and proceeded to roll back the sleeves of his black silk shirt, exposing an expensive Rolex watch on one thick, hairy wrist and a gold chain, together with a huge tattoo of a dragon, on the other. As he passed one beefy hand over his shiny clean-shaven pate the line of diamond rings adorning each finger glinted in the dim light. The barman, after muting the TV behind him, reached through the steel grill that encased the bar and moved the bottles closer.

Demosh flexed his thick shoulders and snapped the cap off the bottle with the practiced ease of a man snapping a twig, pouring a quantity slowly into the glass. His moist fingers closed around the glass, circling it momentarily as if sizing it up, leaving sweaty smudges behind. With a glance at the stack of notes, he raised the glass to his lips, angled his head back on his short thick neck, and knocked back the contents in one short gulp.

"Ah!" said someone at the end of the bar. The exclamation became infectious, sweeping in a murmur around the half-circle of eager spectators. With a calm half-smile, Demosh passed the back of his hand over his thick wet lips and refilled the glass. His huge hand closed again around the little glass and the contents disappeared down his throat in the blink of an eye.

Demosh's hand was steady as he finally poured the contents of the last bottle into the glass. A cheer swept the little gathering as he calmly turned the bottle upside down, verifying that the last dregs had been drained, before setting it next to the other empty bottles lined up on the bar. Beads of moisture popped up on his sloping forehead and he took a pressed handkerchief from his pocket and wiped his brow. His eyes were calm but fixed of focus, as if they were concentrating on a point inside his mind that only he could see. For the fifteenth time that night, Demosh flexed his huge prizefighter's shoulders and lifted the glass. The mouths of all the bystanders hung open as they watched his huge jaw swing open and swallow down the contents of the glass.

Demosh placed his hand on the wad of notes and drew them over, dragging his hand over the polished bar. He counted the notes slowly to make sure the full five thousand was accounted for. With a wink and a nod at the poor dumbstruck stranger who had dared throw the challenge his way, Demosh folded the bills into a roll and pushed them into his hip pocket. Then he stood, slapping his black mailman's cap on his head, and walked slowly out of the bar. A stunned silence followed him as he wound his way through the tables.

Demosh was just stepping over the threshold of the pub when he fell.

Demosh's gangster friends formed a menacing half-circle around his bed at Kenyatta National Hospital where he had been rushed. The hospital orderly waited with a steel trolley.

"You heard the doctor. The man's dead," the nurse pleaded with rising panic. "Please step aside and allow him to be wheeled to the mortuary."

The men remained unmoving, their gazes wooden, staring down at their strongest man, refusing to acknowledge the nurse's plea.

"I am sorry, but I may have to call in security," she said with false bravado. "For the last time, please step aside from the bed."

The group of thick-necked thugs favored her with looks of utter contempt, angled jaws chewing furiously on wads of gum. Skelle, the second-in-command, jerked his head slowly toward the door and they walked silently to the exit. Stares followed them as they passed through the crowded hospital corridors, the patients agog at the polished studded leathers, bulging biceps, and garishly flaunted bling. The men emerged in the parking lot, where they piled into their flashy vehicles, parked haphazardly across designated slots, and noisily drove out of the lot.

&

The funeral cortège of the following day was as flashy as the men who attended it. The cars wound their way slowly through the city streets en route to Lang'ata Cemetery. Demosh's family, flanked fore and aft by the long motorcade, had been herded into a huge Cadillac the gang had hired at ten grand an hour. The massive white casket had been strapped to the roof rack of the navy VW Barbie that Demosh used to drive around town. The boom boxes in the VW's boot were going full blast, the deep bass jarring the peace inside the walls of the roomy casket where the dead gangster was having his last nap. Two outriders on powerful Harley Davidson bikes cleared the traffic ahead, shooing aside the gaping kids who crowded the sidewalks.

A little service was held by the graveside. As the clearly overwhelmed pastor led the gathering through the hymn, the gang members remained with their heads bowed, chewing furiously, at a loss for what to say because they didn't know the lines. The ceremony wound to an end, and as the attendants prepared to lower the deceased into the grave the gang intervened. Skelle opened the lid of the casket so that they could have a last look at their buddy before it was nailed shut.

"I say, you were a true gangster, boy. You need to go in style," Skelle whispered softly to himself, adjusting his friend's Armani suit. From a parked car, Skelle retrieved a portable CD player, which he wedged into the casket beside the deceased's feet. He pressed the play button and Coolio's "See You When You Get There" filled the lace-lined casket.

On cue, Denno, the gang's master locksman, reached into his jacket and pulled out Demosh's heavy silver chain, which he had skillfully relieved the fallen gangster of as they were putting him in the ambulance. With shaking hands—the after-effects of a night-long binge—Denno carefully placed the chain around the neck of the corpse.

As for the huge fellow who was being feted, he remained snuggled in the soft laces, his dark face screwed in a half-frown, his thick lips pouting, his eyes not quite shut. Demosh's expression suggested that he wasn't happy that the grim reaper had taken him in such a cheap fashion after his fast-lane lifestyle; he would have preferred, it seemed, to go out with a little more drama.

As they were preparing to nail the lid shut, Kauzi, one of the gang members, his protruding eyes glazed from excessive weed, elbowed his way forward, yelling at the attendants to wait. He was waving the deceased's expensive cell phone, of which he had deftly relieved Demosh as he had been helped up from the floor of the pub. Kauzi's eyes roved over the expensively dressed corpse, as if debating where to place the cell phone.

"You were one mean bastard, Demosh," Kauzi muttered under his breath. "Always meddling in a job to get your cut, while all the while you sat on your fat ass and let others do all the work." His gaze weighed the value of the clothing and jewellery that the dead gangster was taking with him to the grave. "Always liked freebies, didn't you, old boy? I think you deserved what you got in the end. I for one certainly won't be missing you. In any case, you were kind of crowding the pen, you know. Here, I think you'll be needing this," he said, placing the expensive cell phone in the corpse's hip pocket close to his stiff right hand. "You might need to call that fiery place, where they are surely expecting you with a three-pronged fork, and place a booking for an air-conditioned room. Much as I am tempted to keep the snazzy phone, I don't want you spooking me in my dreams. I'm not ready to join you just yet. I've still got some incomplete business in this world. Someone's got to fill the boots you left, you know," he said with a soft laugh. "Well, good riddance, you old bastard. May your fat ass fry in hell." Kauzi crossed himself as his mother had taught him. "Bon voyage!"

"That was quite a eulogy, Kauzi," said Skelle, after Kauzi retreated from the graveside to join the rest of the mourners.

"Yeah, I liked the guy. I'll miss him a lot."

"You are right. We all will."

After the rites had been completed Skelle slipped the deceased's designer sunglasses over his half-open eyes and nodded at the cemetery attendants, who nailed the casket shut and started the winch to lower it into the gaping hole. Skelle completed the ritual by opening a bottle of Bushmill's to anoint the coffin. The casket duly consecrated, the cemetery attendants began the task of shoveling in the dirt.

He woke with a start. It was pitch-dark, and in the cold stillness he could hear strains of Tupac's "Life Goes On." He opened his eyes and tried to take his bearings, but he felt as if sledgehammers pounded about inside his skull. Dry gauze lined his mouth and throat. His tongue was swollen with thirst, and a surfeit of bile set his stomach walls on fire.

Marshaling his strength, he tried to rise on his elbows to take his bearing, but the splitting headache kept him pinned to his bed. With a sigh he sank back, feeling beads of sweat pop up on his brow and trickle down his temples. Somewhere in the recesses of his strange surroundings Snoop Doggy Dog yapped on, as if making a joke of his predicament.

Christ, where the hell was he? He felt about him with his open palm, trying to make sense of the lacy bed sheets and the strange smells. And as his lungs started to burst in the closed airless place he rummaged in his pocket for his cell phone, his breath hissing out through clenched teeth, sweat soaking into his stiff starched collar.

The gang—excepting Kauzi, who had disappeared earlier in the evening—were seated around a corner table playing high stakes poker. Cans of beer and cigarette ash littered the floor around the table. It was approaching the closing hour and the pub was mostly deserted, save for a couple in the corner and the bored barmaids hovering around, stifling sleepy yawns in their fists. Skelle was shuffling the cards, preparing to issue another hand when the cell phone on the table rang. He deposited the cards on the table, and was reaching out to take the phone when he stumbled back in shock, his face ashen.

"What is it?" chorused the rest of the cardsharps.

"Take a look," whispered Skelle, his eyes wide with horror.

"*What?*" Denno exclaimed, toppling his chair as he fell back from the table.

The men stared open-mouthed at the ringing phone, each

frozen in place. The dead man's name flashed blue on the little screen. Skelle, gathering his courage, reached forward with a trembling finger and pressed the speaker button.

"Hey, why the hell ain't you picking up your phone, you bastard?" Demosh's angry tones filled the suddenly silent bar. "Where the hell is this? I hope this is not some kind of joke, as I'll sure kick some ass bad when I get out of here!" A hushed horror descended upon the table as the men froze in their sweats, faces shining with sweat, wide eyes white and glimmering in the dim light of the bar. "Hey, talk to me, won't you?" Demosh insisted. "You son of a bitch! Speak to me!"

The men stared speechlessly at each other, the poker cards strewn on the table, forgotten.

"I said speak to me, you damn bastard! I know you are there!" yelled the agitated caller. "Pick up the damn phone!"

It was drizzling outside as the gang raced from the table to their cars. The poker game would have no winner.

Meanwhile, as the gang ran about in a scare after the bizarre call, the grave-raiders were busy at work. It was a muddy job, with the drizzling rain showing no sign of abating. All the same, Kauzi and the two crooks he had picked up on River Road were determined that they would haul up the casket, rain or not.

It was dark and deserted in the cemetery at that hour, the rain-washed gravestones showing faintly amongst the bushes. The fence who had approached Kauzi with the job had offered a good price for everything that had gone into the grave minus the corpse. He had been at the funeral, and had seen the casket, the suit, and the bling that the gangster was taking with him to the grave. Struggling to shovel wet mud out of the deep grave, Kauzi reflected on his folly at leaving the expensive cell phone in the dead man's pocket. Burying good money due to some stupid premonition…he was clearly losing his touch. After all these successful jobs he had pulled off, perhaps he was nothing more than an old woman after all, he thought dismally.

The men were covered in mud by the time their spades scraped the wood of the casket.

"Hey, careful there, boys," Kauzi said, switching on a little flashlight, the beam of which was filtered through a white handkerchief. "We don't want to mess up the polish now, do we?"

It took all their combined effort and careful manoeuvring to get the casket out of the grave. Breathing heavily, they sat for a moment by the graveside. One of the boys took out a cigarette and prepared to light up.

"Hey, don't you light a match now," said Kauzi, snatching away the match. "We don't want to attract company now that we are almost done." Glancing over his shoulder, Kauzi confirmed that the pick-up truck was where they had left it—parked in the bushes, waiting to cart away the loot. "Hey, let's get this over with now. We'll have time to rest later," he said, leaping to his feet. Retrieving a little jemmy from the muddied pouch of his dungarees, Kauzi went to work on the lid of the casket. One of the boys held the flashlight steady while the other kept an eye out for unexpected company. Kauzi, musing upon the many treasures that were doubtless buried six feet beneath rotting crosses and gravestones all around them, thought a new career as a grave raider might be just to his taste. Treasures that lay in the dark, awaiting the harvest.

The coffin lid came loose and Kauzi and his cohorts swung it slowly to the side, careful not to muddy anything inside.

The dead man sat up slowly, shaking his head to clear his befuddled mind.

"*Ai...Yawa!*" cried one of the boys, springing back, his hair standing on edge.

The dead man shook his head again and opened his eyes, blinking rapidly to get his bearings, spitting out the strange gauze filling his mouth. "You sure took your sweet time, you *falas!*[45] he snapped, his thick brow knit. "Someone get me a glass of water. Boy, isn't it thirsty over there!"

---

[45] Nairobi street slang for 'idiot.'

HEARSE FOR HIRE

I've always gotten my way, ever since I lay on my back for a farm boy in my village in western Kenya at ten. I took his twenty shillings—his wages for the day's labour—and he left with a smile on his face. And none since have yet accused me of robbery, delighted as they are with the value I provide.

Thirty-two years in the business gives me something to say to those young green-horns who try to catch a man on the strength of their looks alone. While these young things will obligingly get on their backs for anyone who will pay, women in my league have the privilege of choice. Why waste time chasing after sardines when you can live off a big fish for a month? These novices do not understand that patience is a virtue. I take my lesson from the big cats that rule the savanna. Lions select their prey carefully; they take their time stalking their chosen prey, ignoring the rest of the herd. Isn't that why they are kings of the jungle? I have learned from the best, and I've never gone wrong so far.

While I am not as well educated as my younger competition, I speak fairly good English, practicing as I do with a native speaker—my English employer. He likes to discuss the early papers with me as I prepare morning tea. I have now mastered the art of smoothly rolling my tongue around words that trip up these fresh schoolgirls. Education aside, I do have papers that speak to my professional credibility. I have a certificate in cookery and am a trained *ayah*.

These daily English sessions with my boss have sharpened my knowledge of world affairs. I know about global warming, the Middle East crisis, the English Premier League, Al-Qaeda, piracy in the coastal waters off Somalia, and U2's Bono and his campaign to encourage Western countries to write off debts owed by the poor of Africa (who never saw a cent of the money themselves). On any given day I could hold my own in conversation on any topic for five minutes or more with my employer's guests.

In addition I have read *Dreams From My Father*, *Things Fall Apart*, *The Number One Detective Agency*; one of the Harry Potter books—I don't remember which exactly; *Weep Not, Child*; *Animal Farm*; and, of course, the Bible. These books are stacked on my shelf in the servants' quarters, beside a pile of *Cosmopolitan*, *True Love*, and *Readers Digest* that the *mamsaf*[46] had finished browsing. By "reading" I mean that I have labored through a few chapters before sleep overtakes me; enough, though, that I can give my two cents' worth in a conversation on any of these books. If book talk fails, I can dance the salsa, and I know a little about jazz, which I frequently listen to on my employer's stereo. Occasionally, I accompany *Mamsaf* and the kids to the movies. We have seen *Titanic*, *Pirates of the Caribbean*, *Tomb Raider*, *Out of Africa* and a number of others that I can't remember, all while stuffing ourselves with popcorn and sodas—childish food sold at outrageous prices. That makes me a super mama, right? But the icing on the cake, the experience that really elevates me

---

[46] A colonial term by which house servants referred to their mistresses, meaning 'madam.' It is still used occasionally, fifty years after independence, particularly by older servants in the affluent, previously white-only residential neighborhoods of Nairobi.

above these fresh-faced girls, is the fact that I have been to England! I traveled with my United Nations employer on holiday, babysitting for them as they visited family.

I know quite a bit about men, and I know that they will pay top dollar for a pea-brain who is nicely packaged. In this, I knock the competition flat. I buy my clothes from fashionable stores in European cities, and on those specific occasions when I opt for an African look, I depend upon the services of a talented Ghanaian tailor at the Kenyatta market, who imports her fabric. You wouldn't catch me dead in those dead-men's clothes sold at the Gikomba flea market; nor would I buy my shoes from the pile under a street lamp or wear the cheap plastic accessories manufactured in China. My perfume is the real deal, and my hair is styled at the top downtown salons. But the crown jewel is my warm smile. I have a natural gap in my big white front teeth, and when I smile I can make the meanest man's heart melt like butter in a skillet.

So it is, with all these attractions, I am able to lure and keep regulars like the flashy Munir, who takes me to business conferences—a decision that would send his wife searching for a rope and the nearest tree branch if she were to find out. I see my competition gape at those stretch limousines in society magazines and laugh softly to myself—for unlike those greenhorns, I have *ridden* in them. My confident sense of style allows me to walk through the entrance of Tribe Hotel as a booked guest, commanding a smile and a bow from the maître d'. And I never disappoint. I know to keep my mouth shut when the men are talking business, and to massage their bloated egos afterwards as I peel off their dollars.

But perhaps my biggest advantage is that I know the secret to a man's heart: treat him as his mother would. With a full African figure and butter-melting smile, I understand full well that it is the comfort of a warm bosom that lulls a man to sleep. While men might pay to gape at skinny figures in fashion and strip shows, at the end of the day they are just that—shows.

Looking back over my long career, I think I have done society a great favour. While shrinks charge a fortune to have rich folks lie on their couches and tell them about their problems, I charge relatively little to calm nervous CEOs, keeping them sufficiently relaxed to run their companies. Who knows how many dull marriages I have kept going by distracting the head of the house and keeping him happy?

My chosen occupation has its own thrills. Once I dated a big-shot businessman whose wife worked as a newscaster with a local TV station. We used to leave the TV on as we went about the business of peeling the bananas. My client would start dressing by the time the newscasters got to the weather forecast, and by the time the madam got home her husband would be warming their bed, snoring like a meek lamb. Now, *that* was one thrilling set-up. Too bad he got greedy and wanted to put a chain on me.

All the same, I'm well aware of the risk, and I am prepared. I can hold my own in a catfight with a furious missus any day. In fact I wouldn't advise any of those pantywaist sisters—yes, for some reason the wives of most rich folks always look like survivors of a Nazi camp—to dare have a go at me. I am a big African mama who treats her body well—I eat solid food that sits squarely in my belly, and want nothing to do with those five-star hotel's tiny salad portions. I always carve my helpings, and I'm not shy about it. Question is, if all of us were to eat fresh leaves, then what would the goats eat?

Anyway, the goats business aside, I've had a run of good luck so far. I have built upcountry homes for my parents and myself, and put my son—who lives with my parents—through good schools. I have invested in real estate in my hometown upcountry and own shares in two top companies listed at the NSE, thanks to one of my clients. You see, my money doesn't all go to clothes and shoes. With close to half a million shillings in the bank for a rainy day, I have padded the nest well, and, should I need to retire today, I would not starve.

I do not mean to suggest that I am a sophisticated socialite; far from it. Even as I make my money helping powerful, moneyed men with bloated egos to unwind over the weekend, deep down I still harbor simple village tastes. I was, after all, raised in a village, and there is some truth to the saying that while you can take a villager out of the village, it is not so easy to take the village out of him. I may have flown Club class to London, sipped vintage champagne from thin-stemmed, cut-crystal glasses, and spent weekends at exclusive resorts in Watamu and Shela, but I know that I am not one of them.

I occasionally return to Kawangware slums to drink *busaa* from a rusty tin and dance *isukuti*[47] with those who speak my native language in its raw, unfiltered form. Sometimes I spend the weekend at Amukanga's tin-walled shack and prepare his meals and share his narrow bed, and, at the end of

---

[47] A vigorous traditional dance from Western Kenya.

it all, accept his twenty shillings' fare for a *matatu* ride back to my house in the wealthy part of town.

Amukanga is an interesting man. During the day he works as a cook for an Asian family in Parklands. On weekends he dons his long white robe fringed with red and green, together with a skull-cap and thick tortoise-shell spectacles— prescribed by no optician that I know of—and becomes a pastor of the African Divine Church. His pastoral duties often require him to spend the night at the funeral wakes in the slum, overseeing the fund-raising service; however, he doesn't mind losing sleep over these obligations because a percentage of the night's takings usually end up in his briefcase.

Amukanga conducts funerals and weddings and resolves all manner of disputes on behalf of his flock, a good portion of which are engineered by his randy accomplices. For these undertakings he collects a fee, either in cash or in kind. I have occasionally carried his briefcase for him to some of these functions. Inside the tough ox-skin briefcase he keeps a well-thumbed Swahili Bible with a cracked leather cover and an old Oxford Advanced Learner's Dictionary that is falling apart at the spine. The dictionary adds necessary weight, for Amukanga never made it through elementary school. Typically the senior woman in the church hierarchy, the Mama Assembly, takes responsibility for carrying the briefcase, which indicates how highly I rate. Once, Amukanga tried to persuade me to take up a role as the Mama Assembly, but I politely declined.

Amukanga is also the father of my son—something that gives him immense pride, despite the fact that he has never financed anything in the boy's upbringing, save the sponsoring of his circumcision when he came of age. And this isn't to say I hold anything against him. Indeed, he once offered to help, but I firmly declined. His three wives upcountry and their numerous offspring are already a weight upon his purse.

My relationship with Amukanga is as natural as that of a man and a wife. He eats my meals with relish, which makes me very happy, and he takes an immense pride in introducing me to his visitors, which makes me happier still. And in the sack he still plucks a fine tune from the old fiddle, which makes my happiness immeasurable. We go back a long way, he and I. I met him on a job-hunting mission in one of my first trips to the city. The years in between have been a long tale of binge drinking and partying, fierce fights and making up, and innumerable trips to see the *wazee*[48] upcountry.

Throughout the years, we have remained comfortable together, like a hand in a glove. Amukanga remains the only man who can make me feel calm in a crisis. Evenings spent in his company are always golden, whether we are drinking *busaa* from old tins in Congo or drinking bottled beer at Bora Bora and dancing to band music. With Amukanga, unlike my wealthy clients, I never have to pretend, and I have often thought that he would make the perfect husband—if he had money, if he didn't already have three wives. He is also the only man who doesn't have to wear a condom when we are together.

When I discovered how he made his money, however, I was shocked. Not that this revelation wasn't entirely unexpected in this city of many secrets—secrets being something

---

[48] tribal elders

I know much about. What surprised me was that Amukan-ga's schemes had been going on since the day we first met and I had, for so long, known nothing of them.

Late one Friday evening, I'd just returned from a date with Munir at the Serena. Munir's wife was threatening divorce, which would mean a ton of money changing hands and a ton more in monthly maintenance when she took the kids with her. Listening to the figures Munir was reeling off so casually, I decided I was much better off. While these rich folks might have millions in the bank, it would appear that they have zillions of problems trying to keep that money there. All those millions seemed to attract mostly misery and stress, and I concluded that I'd rather remain right where I was—nibbling at the fringes of the pie like a world-wise rat.

As it turned out, the old boy had just wanted someone to talk to. Munir had paid for a room for two, only to change his mind after I had soothed him awhile in my lap and he felt strong enough to face his devils waiting for him at home. I still found it incredible, the money these rich clients would throw around, and the waste of it all—an expensive dinner that was barely eaten, an expensive suite they didn't sleep in. Was it any wonder their women were always scheming how they could get a share of the action for themselves? I wasn't really looking forward to spending Friday night in the company of a sulking millionaire. What mattered to me was what he would tuck in an envelope after the evening was over.

After he had put me in a taxi and left in his custom-made Range Rover, I sat a long while in the back of the cab before asking the cab driver to take me to Kawangware. I had been a little edgy myself over some business with *Mamsaf*. While our misunderstanding was supposedly about a hand-painted porcelain jug that I had accidentally broken the day before, we both knew that *Mamsaf*'s simmering anger was due to the tips and gifts her husband had been giving me. The day before, I caught the *Mzee* staring at my booty as I hoovered the rug in the TV room. By the time Friday evening rolled around, I really needed a good lay with someone who understood me, preferably after a few drinks.

I found Amukanga at Bora Bora in the company of a few of his friends. I always liked to come to the old club in the heart of the slum; it seemed nostalgic, all those drinks and *nyama choma* we had shared in the club over the years. There was a comfort, too, in the fact that everyone knew everyone else, unlike the clientele of the swankier Half London across the road, where beer was sold at the downtown price, and skinny girls carried prescription tranquillizers hidden under long fingernails, waiting to be slipped into someone's glass. The Bora Bora band was playing Luseno's "Mukangala", which suited me just fine. As we waited for the motherly waitress to take our order, Amukanga rose with a disarming smile and held out his hand. I gave him mine and we moved to the dimly lit dance area.

It was midnight before we left the club. Amukanga had pending business upcountry the following morning and didn't want to stay out too late. I stopped to buy half a kilo of tripe and liver from a late-night butchery, and we made our way through the narrow streets, still crowded with drunks.

A funeral wake was taking place a stone's throw from Amukanga's house, and as the area pastor he needed to make an appearance while I prepared supper. There was always a funeral occurring somewhere in the slum, and almost always it was that of an African Divine Church faithful. While Amukanga was away, I prepared the evening meal on his cheap Chinese stove, keeping the flame low to keep it warm. Then I stretched out on his cheap sofa, working my way through the bottle of Richot I had brought with me from the club. At that moment I felt that I was a content African woman waiting for her man to return home from an evening out with the boys.

I must have drifted off to sleep because I didn't hear Amukanga letting himself in. I helped him out of his greatcoat and made him comfortable on the sofa with a glass of Richot. I ladled out the meal and we sat down to eat. He had brought in a carton box and a big bag, which he intended to take with him in the morning.

After the meal was done, I dimmed the lamp and rose, shrugging off my dress and dropping it on the couch. Amukanga gulped down the remainder of his brandy and rose, following me to the bed, which was separated from the sitting area by a Chinese bed sheet decorated with huge blue peacocks.

Our activity woke our neighbor to the right, who wasted no time in seeking the same with his own unwilling partner. When the creaky bedsprings finally fell silent and the sighs were let out on either side of the *mabati* wall, I drifted into a deep, contented sleep.

I was awoken by shuffling feet and a low whistling. Amukanga was already up and had just returned from his cold dousing at the bath shelter in the yard outside. Dressed in his red nylon shirt, with a towel wrapped around his slim hips, he was bending over the cheap nylon suitcase he had brought in the evening before, packing.

I was about to call out a "good morning" but the word died in my throat. Through a parting in the peacock bed sheets, strung from nails in the rafters, I saw a horrifying sight. Had it not been for the shifting light of the kerosene lamp, I might have missed it entirely. The suitcase was crammed full of clothes, presumably ones he was taking with him for the journey, and he was trying to close the zipper and lock the case with the padlock that encircled the handle. Every time he drew one side of the zipper closed, the opposite one would pop open and the lid would spring upwards. It was then that something slid out of the bulging suitcase, and, cursing softly, he hastily crammed it back inside. It was a tiny human hand with five fingers that were short and chubby.

I watched aghast as Amukanga pondered the problem, his chin resting on his hand, his back turned towards me. Then, seemingly reaching a decision, he opened the case and flung back the lid. Inside, covered by a few clothes, was the bloated corpse of a small child, his belly ballooned with gas, and clearly the cause of the problem. Amukanga rolled up his sleeves and, feeling the swollen belly the way a farmer would a well-fed goat up for sale at the local cattle market, spread his hands across the taut skin and leaned heavily upon them. The soft hiss of wind escaping the orifices sounded like a male trombone in a somber Salvation Army band piece.

Amukanga then replaced the clothes atop the corpse, spritzed the contents with a canister of the cheap but strongly scented Yolanda spray, closed the lid, and slid the zippers with ease. After securing the padlock, he rose to his feet and almost caught me peeping, so mortified was I by what I had seen.

"Lorna?" he called softly. "Are you awake?"

I turned over in the bedclothes and purred like a butcher's cat, curling into that embryonic position we of the animal species remember from our short stay in the womb. Amukanga came to the bedside and patted me softly on the shoulder.

"I have to leave now," he murmured. "Don't bother waking up to make me anything; I'll have tea at a kiosk. I will be back tomorrow evening, and will bring you some bananas and cassava from the farm. Meet me here after work, and I'll buy you a drink at Bora Bora." Then he leaned over and kissed me softly on the forehead and pulled the covers over my shoulders.

I shivered, feeling like a child who had discovered monsters under the bed. To conceal my confusion I burrowed deeper into the bedclothes, pretending sleep. I heard the blade rasp on Amukanga's cheeks as he shaved in the doorway, then the sounds of him dressing, and the gentle thud of the wooden door closing softly behind him.

I sprang from the bed, dressing quickly, relieved that I had left behind a thick poncho on a previous visit. On the bedside stool, I noticed he had left a fifty-shilling note for my bus fare, but I ignored it. After ten minutes had elapsed, I left. I already knew where he was headed.

Most of the cheap country buses had cubbyhole offices at Stage Two in Kawangware, having relocated from Machakos Country Bus Station downtown, where they would be obliged to pay the City Council a fee to pick up passengers.

These buses—unlike the more organized, expensive bus companies that had offices in town—were quite convenient for Amukanga's business; there were no security checks to pass through before boarding, whereas the chances of smuggling a corpse in a case on to a town-based Easy Coach or Akamba bus without detection were slim indeed.

I trotted along the deserted sidewalk that would soon be crowded with dried-sardine and *sukuma-wiki* sellers, hugging the poncho around myself. The early risers were already leaving the slum. Young men in twos and fours were trekking to town or wherever it was they toiled for the day's wage. The women traders, clutching gunny sacks, bunched together at *matatu* stops, waiting for the first *matatu* to take them to Wakulima market to buy fresh vegetables. Along the dusty sidewalk, the flames leapt around the sooty frying pans of the *mandazi*[49] sellers as they hurried to prepare breakfast for their customers.

The country buses were lined up like trail hounds that had cut the spoor, straining restlessly on the leash, engines revving loudly as they belched out clouds of black diesel smoke. Bands of touts tried to shepherd the few arriving travelers to the buses whose drivers paid their commission. From behind a shop pillar, I watched Amukanga purchase a ticket from one of the ticketing agents and then walk towards his bus, the bulging suitcase close by his side. One of the elders from the local church, whose name I knew as Shivachi, had joined him. They both wore church skull-caps and operated with a practiced smoothness that suggested they had long been accomplices.

---

[49] triangle-shaped buns

One of the touts offered to stow Amukanga's suitcase on the roof rack but he firmly declined. I had to admire Amukanga's aplomb. He carried himself with all the dignity of a shantytown pastor, his polyester suit crisp from the *dhobi*'s[50] coal iron, and three multicolored Bic biros neatly aligned in his breast pocket. His pastoral briefcase was carried by Shivachi, who might have sprung out of the pages of a fashion magazine from the Sixties, with his bright cravat and wide-lapelled, midriff-hugging tweed *mutumba* suit. I watched until they took their seats, the suitcase, with its macabre secret, stowed under the seat in front. It was an ingenious scheme—two church elders off on some church business upcountry. It was highly unlikely that a cop would stop them to ask their business or solicit a bribe.

Later that morning, as soon as I had seen my boss and the missus off to work, I settled myself by their bedroom phone. One of the unwritten perks that accompanied working as house-help for UN expats was that they footed all the phone bills their staff accumulated while trading gossip with friends after they had left for work; it was an old rule, but one cast in stone. For some time, I speculated on the handful of chatty women from Kawangware, wondering whom to call, before deciding on Ezina, the choir soloist who worked as an ayah in Spring Valley. I could hear her surprise when we finally got to the subject on my mind, after all the necessary small talk about employers, husbands, exes, boyfriends, friends' boyfriends, and so on.

"You mean you've never known what Amukanga does all these years?" she asked in disbelief. "Well, you must be

---

[50] a washer of public laundry/ launderer

the dumb ear of Kawangware. And I thought you and he shared a blanket occasionally?" A burst of chortling laughter exploded from the earpiece.

Well, the short of it—or so I learned from Ezina—was that Amukanga worked in cahoots with Shivachi, and another younger man called Ambunya, as undertakers or hearses for hire, servicing Kawangware residents who could not afford to bury their dead at the City Council cemetery in Lang'ata or transport them upcountry by conventional hearses. Amukanga's fee for this service depended upon the size of the body. In addition to bus fare and an allowance for travel refreshments, a body that fitted in a thermos flask carton—anywhere from a fetus to a six-month-old baby—cost two thousand shillings to deliver. A pressure-lamp carton of bigger size cost three thousand shillings. Chinese suitcases, then, came in an additional range of sizes, each costing incrementally a thousand more.

The business had its share of mishaps. The trio had once transported the body of a twelve-year-old boy in a huge metal trunk, but after the conductor dropped the trunk while lowering it from the roof rack, they decided to place a size limit on future jobs. Although the lid, fortunately, didn't burst open, the poor fellow inside was jolted rather badly. The dead, apparently, have feelings that the undertaker respects.

On another occasion they sat the body of a grown woman in the seat next to the driver, covering her with a *khanga*.[51] While the front seat was conveniently easy to access, the drawback was that the scent of body rot would disseminate faster next to the heat of the engine. Amukanga and

---

[51] loin-cloth made of cotton

his accomplices strategically took up seats around the dead woman, preventing the other passengers from getting close enough to sniff the morgue fluids. Transporting a corpse by public transport was, after all, a chargeable offence. The journey was not without incident. The bus was stopped at a roadblock by cops seeking thieves who had escaped using a public service vehicle after robbing a cash-in-transit van. Everyone was required to get off the bus for a body search. When the cops asked why the woman in the front had not left the bus, the conductor explained that she was ill. Fortunately for Amukanga when the cop went to investigate, the corpse's head slipped forward, as if she were drooping in sleep. The cop withdrew and the bus crew again covered her with the *khanga*. When Amukanga and his accomplices finally offloaded the body into a pickup truck in a dark backstreet in Kakamega town, the bus crew, who had been part of the deal, demanded extra pay for handling the tense business with the police.

In addition to transporting corpses, the enterprising trio also conducted burials and disposals—in the case of aborted or still-born fetuses. Since it cost a small fortune to bury ones dead in Lang'ata Cemetery, Amukanga and his band accepted a fraction of the fee to do the job at the disused City Council cemetery across the valley at '84 in Kangemi. The City Council had closed the '84 cemetery because if you scratched the surface more than one foot deep at any spot in the trash-strewn field you would most likely disturb a fellow who was resting in his heavenly peace with the maggots.

Under cover of darkness, Amukanga and his gang would creep into the overgrown graveyard carrying a bundle and a little hoe; shortly thereafter, they would leave behind a little mound of fresh earth that the next downpour would promptly uncover. But by then they would have long since collected their pay, the tears would have dried on the faces of the bereft, and memories would have faded. The tiny fetuses were simply dropped in the brown river for the mudfish to finish off—for wasn't that the watery equivalent of the job the grubs completed under the earth?

By the time I hung up the phone I had grown substantially wiser in the ways of the world. My mind worked through the details as Ezina had relayed them, and I found that I no longer condemned Amukanga for his deeds. At the end of the day someone had to dispose of the dead, and unlike the funeral homes, Amukanga didn't charge an arm and a leg for his services. And being a man of God, he ensured that each customer was dispatched with full honours and ceremony.

The truth of it was that I didn't exactly live a pious life myself, and now that I was an accomplice, by virtue of occasionally sharing in the profits of the business, I might as well offer a hand. I made a mental note to get Amukanga a bottle of my employer's Brut Fabergé to replace the Yolanda. Brut would certainly smell better on his fares. It also occurred to me, surprised as I was at the revelation, that I looked forward to my promised drink at Bora Bora when Amukanga returned.

THE SWINDLE

Abu walked with a slouch, in a well-practiced rolling street gait, the heels of his thick white Adidas sneakers just barely making contact with the ground. He wore his NY Knicks cap at an angle over his right ear and his heavy shiny "bling" chain—adorned with a heavy crucifix—hanging all the way down to his navel. A row of multicolored stones glinted from rings that adorned four fingers of his right hand, and which, in other circumstances, served as effective knuckle-dusters. Diamond studs gleamed in his ears with every swing of his head. With his right arm slightly bent at the elbow and his palm cupped—as if ready to scoop up some overlooked treasure—he might have been rolling along on a basketball rink in a Brooklyn neighborhood. It was, all in all, the carefully mastered walk of a "yoyo."

Abu was flanked by the Kirinyaga Road rat on one side—a little man in a worn corduroy jacket with canvas patches on the elbows and a frayed newsboy's cap—and his mechanic on the other, carrying the samples wrapped up in a greasy newspaper parcel. The rat moved with a rapid, shuffling walk that enabled him to navigate his way around people's elbows, greeting street-side acquaintances with a cursory wink or a furtive tap on the shoulder as he passed.

From beneath the lowered rim of his cap, the rat's bright dark eyes constantly moved, surveying the crowds, his manner pleasant, his lips spread in a ready grin, revealing browned teeth. The only characteristic of his companion that mattered to Abu, however, was that the little city man was completely in awe of Abu's 'yoyo' act.

Although Abu had initially been uncomfortable at his mechanic's suggestion that they seek vehicle spares in this part of town, he quickly warmed to the idea once they arrived. The jostling crowds of downtown Nairobi were imbued with a sense of purpose. Time was of the essence; these city people didn't have time to waste idling around and were focused on getting the job done before tackling the next one. It was a hustler's paradise, a Mecca of sorts for the serious scammer wannabe. And there was safety in numbers.

In Mombasa, where Abu had lived all his life, things were different. People went about their business with an embellished panache, whether they were buying a shirt, eating a meal, making love, or even taking a crap. There was an unhurried ritualism to almost all aspects of life (*mdogo mdogo*)[52] and commercial connections were carefully and cautiously made. In Nairobi, however, business alliances were easily struck and just as easily broken up. Although strange to "a coastal" like Abu, this experience was not unpleasant. He was a hustler now and had determined that he'd better learn to roll along Nairobi-style.

As they made their way down the street Abu glanced at his watch, a flashy diamond-encrusted *bijou* which had cost a small fortune in a Dubai store that specialized in the finest imitations.

"Hey, wazzup yo guys? Hurry up with this, will ya? I'm getting late," Abu said in a Brooklyn drawl, a frown mar-

---

[52] bit by bit; literally "slow slow."

ring his baby-soft Jay-Z face that was just starting to sprout a beard. Abu's pulpy pink lips, highlighted with a dash of lipstick, protruded like a woman's as a result of the grillz he wore on his teeth. A country man wouldn't have understood a word of what he said.

"Ah, don't worry, brother," said the rat, with the best imitation of Abu's twang that his Kirinyaga Road-bred tongue could manage, flashing his companion a bright grin. "Everything will go *chap chap*," he added with a snap of the finger. The rat had watched enough gangster-rap videos in Nairobi *matatus* to be fairly confident in his swagger and tone. His darting eyes had already assessed the watch in the brief moment that Abu had lifted the sleeve of his dazzling white Eckó T-shirt, though his face gave nothing away. "You must be very busy, eh?" he added as way of conversation.

"Wazzat?" said Abu, his frown deepening.

"Busy…busy…" said the rat with an elaborate flick of his hand.

"Oh, yeah… Busy as hell, man," Abu drawled. "I operate a fleet, man, a fle-et. Know what that is?"

"*Phew*! It must be tough work," the rat acknowledged with an air of bewildered eagerness.

"I tell you, you ain't seen half of it. It ain't like running a *jua-kali* kiosk,[53] man. You need to be on your toes all the time, beating schedules and deadlines and stuff, you know what I mean?" Abu's fingers snapped like pistol shots, sharply punctuating his speech. "You either hustle with the flow,

---

[53] Literally "open sun," referring to the kiosk- or shed-based little enterprises that occupy the lower-end workers in Kenya's economy; enterprises that don't require much capital to start, and which bring in just enough to put bread on the table.

or you lose business, man."

"*Phe-e-ew!*" whistled the rat, impressed.

"I tell you, you ain't seen nothin', man!" added Abu, as triumphantly as a choir master who has successfully pulled off a high starting note. "And hey, yo! What's your name?" he asked, patting the little man on the shoulder.

"Kiki," the rat replied, baring his mouthful of rotten teeth.

"Funny name," said Abu with a chuckle, skirting around a handcart laden with greasy gunnysacks of scavenged scrap. "Had a dog in ma neighborhood with a name like that."

The broker laughed good-naturedly at the joke. "Just ask for Kiki. Anyone on Kirinyaga Road will tell you where I am. They know me all the way to the Industrial Area," he said proudly.

"Oh, really?" said Abu with a raised eyebrow.

"Sure, man," said the little man cheerfully. "All the *Wahindi* in the spares business know Kiki. Why, if you ask the street kids, even they'll bring you right to where I am!"

"I bet they would too," Abu said with a chuckle. "Seems like every dude on the street knows you."

"Man, Kiki is famous, I tell you," said the little man, fairly bursting with pride. "Ask in Nyamakima, Ngara, Eastleigh… all those places. Everyone knows Kiki. It is the reason your mechanic came to me."

"Is that so, Rama?" said Abu, turning to his mechanic, who seemed preoccupied with the problems that needed fixing in the two buses in the garage. He wasn't much of a talker by nature.

"He's right, boss," said Rama. "He sure is famous; but only on Kirinyaga Road."

The broker laughed good-naturedly. "See? I can even stand for Governor. These people will elect me!"

"Ow, really?" said Abu, baring his grillz in a grin. "I bet ya would, too. You can charm a snake!"

"And what's your name, boss?" the rat asked, emboldened by the easy camaraderie he had managed to whip up.

"My name?" Abu said, scratching his head daintily with a manicured finger. "Ma boys call me Boo-Gee. That's my name."

"Yeah, man," said the rat with a bobbing nod, imitating Abu's drawl. "And you're a cool dude, too."

"Real cool, man...just ask ma boys back in the 'hood, they'll tell you Boo-Gee is a real cool brother!" Abu proclaimed, evidently pleased at the impression he had made on the little city man. "When I've made a good round trip from the coast and back and the dough's in, ma boys know that I throw a party like a real gangsta....I splash the *G*'s around, man, wow! Feels great, I tell ya!"

"Really?" said the rat, his eyes aglow.

"Man, you ain't seen nothin', I told ya!" Abu said with a throaty laugh, slapping the little man on the shoulder. "You should come down to the coast someday, man... I tell ya!"

"*Phe-e-ew,*" mused the rat, shaking his head, reminded that it had been several days since his last solid meal. Kiki's belly rumbled as he imagined a plate full of roast chicken and *pilau* [54] rice, washed down by a gallon or two of beer.

They walked on for a while in silence until they arrived at the end of the street, near the Race Course Road junction.

---

[54] Spicy rice, cooked with cloves, bits of meat, and exotic condiments, popular along the Kenyan coast, especially during wedding feasts.

There Kiki stopped next to the disused public toilet. "We are here," he said, indicating a little side alley that departed from the busy street.

"What?" said Abu, surprised.

"Easy," said the rat with his infectious smile. "Relax, brother. This is just the front office. The store is at the back of the street."

"Your office is in a public toilet?"

"Not a toilet, Abu. It is a base. A front office," said the broker earnestly, his moist face suddenly anxious. A couple of street kids lounged against the graffiti-covered wall of the commandeered City Council toilet, plastic bottles half full of industrial adhesive stuck to their upper lips. The broker made a face at them and they scattered into the traffic, their oily gunny sacks slung across their shoulders.

"Well, where's the merchandise then?" Abu asked impatiently. "I am a busy man, y'know," he added, with a glance at his flashy watch. "I've got two full bookings waiting for me. I don't have all day to waste."

"In a moment, Abu," said the broker. "But first I need the samples in order to get the right parts from the shop. It's right at the back, through the corridor. It will just take a minute, and I'll give you a bargain that you'd never get with anyone else on this street; that is my guarantee."

"Wa...wa...wait," Abu protested as the broker reached for the newspaper bundle the mechanic was carrying. A hint of alarm showed in the depths of his eyes. "You mean we trust you with the samples just like that? What if you disappear with them?"

"Now, boss, there's something here which I think you do

not understand," said the broker, his mouth curling in an infectious grin like that of a prankish elf in a bedtime tale. "Please let us understand each other. As I told you, all the dealers on this street know me. I have worked here since I was a kid. This is where I get the money to feed my family; this is where I get my *unga*. I have no other job, and I depend on customers like you to bring me business. I cannot pretend to own any of these stores," he said, waving his arms to encompass the myriad cubbyhole stores that lined the street, selling auto spares. "These stores are owned by the *Wahindi*, and my arrangement with them is simple. I bring them business, and they give me a cut.

"They trust me to bring them big-shot customers like you, and they give me a handsome bargain. *You* could never get a bargain like that if you haggled all day. But the *Wahindi* say I must not go up to the front counter because then other customers will overhear our prices and demand the same discount. Now, do you understand why I have to conduct my business from the back of the store? No, my friend," the broker continued, taking Abu by the hand. "Any dealer on this street will tell you that the moment you start playing dirty in this business you are sunk. All the customers will vanish into thin air and you will never be able to do business again."

"I see," said Abu, nodding slowly as the little man wound up his animated chatter. "If that is the case then I will give you the samples. But I will not part with any cash until I see the new parts. What do you think, Rama?" he said, turning to the mechanic.

"Sounds fine to me," said the mechanic with a nod. "We

only give him the money after we've seen the new spares."

"Of course," the broker agreed, his face lighting up. "I assure you the parts will be genuine Mitsubishi, and you will have no problem with them. My business partner will help me find the right parts. The *Wahindi* stock both genuine and fake parts, and which you get depends on how much you want to spend."

"As I told you, money is no problem to me, boy, un'er-stand? Man, you truly don't know Boo-Gee," Abu said, re-verting to the drawl that had momentarily slipped him. "I deal only in genuine parts. I'll pay top dollar for good parts. I take nothing short of that, un'erstood?"

"And genuine you will get," said the broker, nodding ear-nestly.

Kiki whistled and a lanky man in drab, grease-streaked dungarees emerged from the alley. His sleeves were rolled up, and several wrenches poked out of his back pocket. In all attributes, save his height—for he was tall and gangly where Kiki was short and solid—he was a carbon copy of the bro-ker, having the same pointed chin, shifty eyes, and disarming smile.

"This here is Ng'ang'a, or simply Ng'ash," said the broker, laying the greasy newspaper upon the ground and unwrap-ping the samples. "Now, Ng'ash, come help me sort out these friends of mine. They need Mitsubishi parts urgently."

Ng'ang'a got down on his knees to examine the parts. He picked up a brake pad and examined it carefully; then a fan belt, to which he gave the same scrutiny before nodding up at his accomplice. "Mitsubishi Coaster," he said. "A luxury vehicle."

"Do we still have all the stocks?" the broker asked.

Ng'ang'a nodded, smiling.

"I say, hurry this up, will you?" Abu muttered, glancing again at his watch. "How much will they cost?"

The broker started folding the samples back into their greasy parcel. His accomplice whipped a small notepad from the kangaroo pouch sewn to the front of his dungarees and started adding up figures using a stub of a pencil that had been tucked behind his ear. Ng'ang'a finished the math and handed the slip of paper to the broker, who pored over the columns briefly before handing the note to their client.

"This is outrageous!" said Abu after a brief glance at the figures. "You mean a single bush goes for this much? Shit, man! You think I'm some kind of fool or what?"

"You said you wanted genuine, didn't you?" said the broker, licking his lips nervously. "That is the cheapest price we can get those parts for, brother. These are luxury brands—"

"I know that," said Abu irritably. "I know what kind of vehicles I got in my fleet, or do you think I'm a fuckin' moron?"

"Sorry, brother," Kiki apologized. "Alternatively, we can try the other option…"

"No, don't even think of it," said Abu, wagging a fat finger. "I told you, I don't touch fakes, man. I don't touch that fuckin' shit."

"Well…" The broker shrugged, licking his lips anxiously as he waited.

In the end Abu had little choice but to reluctantly agree, and as the two brokers hurried into the corridor he glanced again at his watch and pulled out a perfumed white handkerchief to wipe his brow. The mechanic, who had been quiet all this while, began to speak, but Abu waved him to silence. "Keep your eyes on those two, will you?" he snapped. "That's what I'm paying you for."

Shortly Ng'ang'a and the broker reappeared. Kiki held a little carton box under one arm, while his lanky companion carried a stack of heavy boxes, all bearing the Mitsubishi three-diamond logo.

"Sorry I kept you waiting," Kiki said apologetically, after he had hurried across the street. "These parts were stacked right at the back of the store. Here, have a look at this," he said, handing Abu his carton. "I told you it was genuine stuff from Japan. See for yourself."

Abu opened the carton and reached inside the nylon wrapping. He pulled out an oil filter and held it up to the sunlight. The broker watched him carefully as he examined the part, noting the satisfaction on his face.

"See? I told you. Kiki knows his business, brother," said the broker, with a broad smile.

"Wait. Let ma boy here have a look at it," said Abu, passing the part to the mechanic, who scrutinized it carefully, pausing now and again to tap his thumb nail on the shiny metal canister.

"Genuine," the mechanic pronounced at length, nodding.

"Well, let's have the rest of the stuff then," said Abu with a sigh, dabbing at his moist cheeks with the now soiled handkerchief.

"The cash, boss," said the broker, whipping out a receipt book. "You have seen the goods. They are what you wanted, isn't it?"

Only then did Abu notice that the broker's accomplice, Ng'ang'a, still held the heavy cartons on the far side of the busy street, as if waiting for final instructions.

"You see that *Mhindi* over there?" Kiki said, pointing toward the shop next to the alleyway. Abu followed his gaze and saw a stocky, stern-faced Asian trader; he leaned against his shop counter, jaws working furiously as he ate his way through several bundles of *tambuu* [55] leaves, watching them. "That is the owner of the store," said Kiki. "His name is Samijee. As we are speaking he is waiting for the money so that he can give the okay for Ng'ang'a to hand over the stuff. He cannot release the parts until he sees the money."

"What kinda fuckin' shit set-up is that?" Abu said irritably.

"Samijee allowed us to bring one of the parts because he believes we are doing genuine business, but he wants to make sure you are not a fraudster who might try to pull a fast one on him once he has released the merchandise. That's why he must see your cash first."

"You mean the *Mhindi* thinks I'm some kinda con?" asked Abu, bristling. "Look, man, I've got cash—loads of it. See? And I'm paying every damn penny that I owe for the parts this very minute…in cash, un'erstood?" He whipped out a fat gator-skin wallet which he shook in the face of the broker. "What does tha' mothafucker *Mhindi* think I am, huh?"

Kiki took a step back and waited, eyes lowered. At the shop counter the Asian trader leaned over to spit onto the dusty pavement before taking a fresh leaf from the bundle.

---

[55] A stimulant chewed mostly by Asian men in Nairobi; a bunch of bitter-tasting leaves in which are wrapped a blend of grated traditional herbs. It gives the chewer a high and often causes them to become irritable and their eyes bloodshot.

His eyes, red-rimmed from the stimulant, were fixed upon the four men.

"Well, you can always go to the counter yourself and buy directly from him," Kiki said with a shrug. "Samijee will be very glad to sell to you at the counter price, you know."

"All right, write the damn receipt," Abu snapped, counting out the money. "Boo-Gee has more important business to do, man. There's no fuckin' time to waste bargaining with fuckin' *Wahindi.*"

The broker counted the money twice before stowing the wad away in his coat pocket. Then, wetting his thumb, he opened a fresh page in his receipt book, lining the carbon paper carefully between the receipt and the copy. "Please confirm that all the entries are correct," Kiki requested, after he had carefully entered all the items.

Abu glanced quickly at the receipt before nodding. "Hurry it up, man, will ya?"

"One minute, please. Let me give the money to the *Mhindi* so that he can allow Ng'ang'a to bring the rest of the merchandise. Do you want that packaged up for you?" the beaming broker asked, indicating the oil filter which the mechanic was still holding.

"Sure. And hurry it up, dammit!"

"One minute, *bwana.* I will have everything wrapped carefully, together with your samples."

Kiki whistled shrilly and Ng'ang'a started in their direction. The broker started towards the shop counter as Abu called to his mechanic, "Come on, let's go get the stuff and get on our way."

When both parties were midway across the crowded street

Kiki broke into a run, darting effortlessly into the traffic, weaving between cars. Abu turned slowly, like a man in a trance, and saw Ng'ang'a drop the cartons, which spilled bricks onto the ground, before he too disappeared down the alley. These events transpired so rapidly and so casually that very few people on the street—save the ubiquitous fellow brokers—noticed.

It took a moment for Abu to recover his wits, after which, in a fit of rage, he took off after the con, dodging cans and rotting cabbages that littered the narrow urine-bathed alley. This was his second mistake of the day in the big bad city.

Halfway down the alley, Abu sensed a presence jogging beside him; a battered size fourteen Nike sneaker easily kept pace to his right. Turning to examine the new arrival, he felt a sharp pain in the ribs as knobbed knuckles prodded him on.

"*Cheka na mimi…changamka, jo!*"[56] A whiff of cheap home-made liquor wafted from between a row of crooked brown teeth that glinted in the dark alley like a roasted corn-cob.

Breathing hard, Abu stopped and began to swivel, seeking the help of his mechanic. A thick arm swung over his head, and locked in place beneath his chin. The blood rushed to his head as the stranger, who must have been seven feet tall, applied the *ngeta*[57] squeeze. Abu felt his limbs flailing help-lessly in the air.

---

[56] Street slang, literally translating as: 'Laugh alongside me; cheer up, man!' It is a phrase a mugger might use ironically to one they are about to rob.

[57] A mugging technique common on Nairobi streets where the mugger holds his victim in a hammerlock, lifting him off the ground. A wooden bar strapped to the inside of his arm chokes the victim, forcing him to comply, as an accomplice empties his pockets, taking his jewelry, shoes, and other attractive items.

While thick meaty hands held him high above the ground, the fingers that worked their way deftly through his pockets were slender and spidery, even polite—the sort of fingers that are quite accustomed to slipping in and out of narrow crevices, and extracting things discreetly with practiced ease.

"*Hiyo mongolio, jo,*"[58] the giant hissed at his slender-fingered accomplice. "*Pamoja na bling na ndula.*"[59]

It took precisely twenty-five seconds to strip Abu clean of anything that could change hands quickly for *chinky*. When he regained his senses he found himself leaning against the wall, the smell of urine strong in his nostrils, a tender spot in his throat where the narrow wooden bar strapped to the giant's inner arm had bruised his windpipe. The alley was deserted, except for his mechanic at the street entrance, still reeling from a full-handed slap in the face that had almost blinded him.

The end of the alley overlooked the sluggish Nairobi River, which swirled its way slowly downstream, laboring to wash away mountains of city filth that piled upon its banks. A scrawny ibis paused midstream, eyeing Abu malevolently with its glassy eye as it balanced one foot on a piece of rusty piping stuck in the reeds. The bird might have wondered what the barefoot stranger wanted in that dark part of town, disturbing the silence of those that made manure. Then it went back to the more important task of trying to salvage something to eat from the muck.

---

[58] "Take that cellphone."
[59] "Together with the bling and shoes."

VENDING

The three *mama mboga*[60] women slogged their way slowly up the incline, chatting noisily. The women were short and squat, their gingham aprons well-worn and stained with earth and green leaves. Each boasted a massive kangaroo pouch—patched at the front of her apron and filled with house keys, loose change, and other bric-a-brac—which swayed left and right with each movement of her large, pendulous breasts. Massive baskets, fashioned from old jute bags, rested heavy on their backs, held in place by a thick strap that passed across their foreheads. With farm-coarsened hands, the women maintained a firm grip on the straps as they inched on, heads lowered so that they could barely see the road ahead.

The baskets were piled high with an assortment of green vegetables, freshly harvested from their farms down in the valley. Despite their sizeable loads, the women found time to stop once in a while to laugh heartily at a joke or a piece of juicy gossip, their lined and rounded faces glowing with mirth, stocky midriffs shaking. "*Ngai!*"[61] or "*Auuuuwii!*" one or another would exclaim with a hoot of laughter. Then they'd wipe their teary eyes and resume their slogging walk. So absorbed were they in their sociable chatter that they were frequently oblivious of the early afternoon traffic that rattled and roared down the road beside them. Occasionally an on-coming motorist blasted his horn when they drifted into the

[60] women vegetable vendors, literally 'vegetable mamas'
[61] Gikuyu for 'God'

roadway, and the women would leisurely move aside, their banter scarcely interrupted.

When they reached First Parklands Avenue they took up their chant as if on cue. "*Iko kitungulu!*" the first said, to which the next picked up, "*...hoho!*" and the last, "*...na kindu kiingi!*" It was an amusing pitch for a warm Saturday afternoon, and it had the cheerful exuberance of a schoolyard rhyme. "*Iko kitungulu...hoho...na kindu kiingi!*"[62]

The three women trudged slowly up the road, pausing to announce their passing to the compounds lining either side, where residents lounged in the shade of their verandahs after their afternoon meal. The guards at the compound gates knew these three, and many at their posts returned the women's lively greetings.

It was the last Saturday of the month, and the three *mama mboga* women were secretly excited, for this was the day when the women of the households, in this predominantly Asian neighbourhood, met for their monthly *chama*, usually at the temple or the home of one of the more prominent families. On occasions such as these, impending weddings or social functions were planned, or, if none was scheduled, the women were content to simply trade the latest gossip as they enjoyed the feast they had prepared. The *chama* was a female-only affair, and the men who were not at work were expected to find other engagements with which to entertain themselves. The monthly *chama* was a tradition that went back to the days when Parklands and Ngara were still considered prestigious neighbourhoods, when the City Council still swept and hosed down the streets and emptied the garbage cans.

---

[62] Get your onions ...capsicums...and other extras!

The *mama mboga* women had heard that an important wedding was to be held in the community. Perhaps today they would enjoy brisk vegetable sales with the promise of the upcoming festivities. As they crossed a junction and passed several compound gates, one of the women, a light-skinned vendor by the name of Njoki, lagged behind. The other two proceeded at a steady pace, heads bent low with the great weights they bore on their backs, between them taking up the portion of Njoki's sales chant. *"Iko kitungulu…hoho…na kindu kiingi!"*

Njoki lowered her basket to the ground and approached a guard lounging in a battered wicker chair in the shade of a dusty frangipani tree. A mangy African bush dog, lying at the guard's feet, opened one rheumy eye to regard the visitor, then went back to a twitchy sleep.

"Jambo,[63] Abedi," said Njoki, revealing her brown-stained teeth in a broad, knowing smile. Delving into her pouch, she withdrew half a roasted maize cob wrapped in leaves and passed it to him through the bars of the wrought-iron gate. The guard, springing awake, hurried to collect his gift and tucked it into his faded nylon tunic so that it would not be seen by his employer. "Is *Mzee* in?"

The guard nodded, a smile flashing across his dark face. The cement drive beyond the gate curved around to an old storied building tucked into a grove of giant mango trees. Paint peeled in long strips off the wooden shutters that framed dusty windows. The original owners had come from India to build the 'Lunatic Express' railway line many years

---

[63] Swahili for 'Greetings!'

before, and it seemed likely the house was as old as the now-rusted railway. Through the golden shower vines clinging to the gate on the balcony that jutted over the carved wooden door, Njoki saw a figure in an old rocking chair.

"Voo is it, Abedi?" the elderly Asian man called, rising from his chair and leaning over the curved balustrade. He wore a singlet and shorts, his heavy biceps and hairy forearms shiny with sweat. He squinted in the bright afternoon sun, his thick eyebrows faded grey, as were the tufts of hair jutting from his bulbous nose. "*Nani iko?*"[64]

"It is mama *mboga*, Mzee," said the guard.

"Ve-ell, *fungulia yeye!*"[65]

Njoki swung the heavy bag onto her back with practiced ease, winking at the guard as he swung the gates open to admit her into the compound. The homeowner, Sailesh, watched her approach, leaning against the balustrade. When she passed out of view beyond the side of the house, he put on his leather slippers and came down to open the back door for her.

"Va-at have you broot toodeh, Njoki?" Sailesh asked with a wide grin, opening the kitchen door and ushering her inside.

"*Kitungulu, hoho…na kindu kiingi*," said Njoki, lowering her bag to the polished terrazzo floor.

"Ve-ell..veell," said Sailesh, cupping her ample backside in his huge hands while she bent over, engaged in freeing the carrying strap from over her head.

"*Ngai!*" said Njoki, making a play of knocking his hands

---

[64] bastardized Swahili for 'Who is there?'
[65] bastardized Swahili for 'open for her'

off her. But then they were both laughing. "Can't a woman have a glass of water first in this hot sun?"

"Ah, that can vaaait," said Sailesh, pulling her into his bear hug.

"You have been eating too much of that *tambuu* of yours again," she said, patting him on the chin. "Your eyes are all red."

"Ve-ell, not too much," said Sailesh, passing a hand behind her back and urging her toward the stairs. "I voos vaaiting for you!"

An ancient air conditioner hummed like a World War One plane above the wide kitchen window, but the air was warm and muggy. The old wooden stairs squealed in protest as Sailesh and Njoki walked arm in arm up to the landing, toward the bedrooms. The guest bedroom, like the other rooms in the house, had a high ceiling with thick layers of cracked and peeling paint. While gleaming glass and steel towers were being erected all over the neighborhood, Sailesh's old house retained a comfortable warmth that modern architecture couldn't match. The memories and secrets of generations of his family were here, embedded in the pits and cracks of the walls and ceilings.

Njoki took off her *lesso* and spread it on the wide bed. Then she reached behind her to free a button, allowing her gown to slip to the floor. All the while Sailesh, having long shed his own clothes, groped her, his eyes closed, his breath warm on her skin. She climbed onto the bed and lay on her stomach, the pillows arranged under her crotch. He liked Indian-style sex best, she knew.

Later, they lay on their backs staring up at the rickety ceiling fan that sluggishly beat warm air over their cooling bodies. Sailesh had broken wind on the crest of the hill, and the odor lingered still in the room. Njoki passed her hand idly over his chest and belly, running her fingers through his pelt of body hair. "You never seem to age, Babur," she said coyly, addressing him by his childhood nickname, one derived from an ancient Indian warrior king. "You are a wicked old lion!"

"And you are my lioness," Sailesh growled, eyeing her with a slanted gaze, his huge teeth flashing.

When Njoki left a short while later her bag was considerably lightened; the assorted peppers, carrots, *dhania*,[66] and cauliflower had been left on the kitchen table for the missus to sort through when she returned from the *chama*.

The three vendors sat in the shade of a gnarled flame tree in the City Park, taking stock of the day's takings. It was evening and the park was gradually filling up with necking couples and strolling families who couldn't afford the fancy city restaurants. Up in the trees the monkeys flashed white and grey as they leapt from branch to branch, their chatter dulling the metallic grind of the endless city traffic on the adjacent road.

Njoki spread her *lesso* on the leaf-strewn ground and sat upon it, her legs akimbo. As she untied the knot in her headscarf, a smile wreathed her lined face.

"Not so bad business today, eh, Njoki?" Waĉeke asked, her browned teeth bared in a gleeful smile.

"You can tell from her eyes," said the third. "The *kuhoya*

---

[66] coriander

hoya[67] was not in vain today."

The three women hummed to themselves as they counted their money. Njoki thought of her block of tin shanties in the Githogoro slums where the three of them lived. She was pulling them down, one room at a time, as the *fundis*[68] converted them into permanent stone-walled rooms that attracted better rent. With today's takings Njoki had enough to cover a truck of sand and three bags of cement.

Across the park the Council worker who had been cutting long grass with a *panga*[69] paused to enviously regard the three women, who always stopped under the flame tree to count their money. His own hustles—mostly bribes from teenagers found in "compromising positions" behind the overgrown bushes—never seemed to raise as much money.

---

[67] Gikuyu for "hustling"; any small-time business enterprise that ordinary folks engage in to put food on the table.
[68] Swahili for "craftsman." Could refer to any skilled craftsman—a mason, tailor, watch-repairman, electrician, or even plumber.
[69] machete

CRUCIFIXION

The faithful at Nyambari Parish Catholic Church should have been slightly alarmed that their new priest had not been formally introduced to them by their trusted, long-serving priest; neither had their priest of fifteen years hinted at his upcoming transfer during recent sermons. They should also have been somewhat suspicious that the new cleric arrived with his own altar boys in tow. The faithful, however, were neither alarmed nor suspicious, largely due to the boisterous charm and charisma of their new man of God. With benevolent, paternal features and neatly combed hair, the new priest was an immediate comfort to the parishioners as he stood—nearly six feet tall—behind the lectern in his fine silk robes, an old-fashioned monocle perched over one eye.

At the priest's signal the old organ player launched into an Easter hymn, "I am the Bread of Life," and the flock rose obediently to their feet. The choir knew the opening notes of the hymn and joined in, their voices rising in flawless accord:

I Am the Bread of Life
You who come to Me shall not hunger
And who Believe in Me shall not thirst
No one can come to Me unless the Father Beckons

The priest's voice rose powerfully above the organ music as he led the Mass into the soulful chorus:

And I will Raise You Up
And I Will Raise You Up

And I will Raise You Up on the Last Day

The church was crammed, and Sunday-goers spilled out into the yard at the front of the church, where speakers, mounted in the trees, intoned the Mass for those who were unable to see the pulpit. The priest proceeded to bless the congregation, and to drink from the holy cup, after which he blessed the Bible and the rosary—the latter which was made of pure gold, like the band on his right ring finger. When the blessings were done, the benevolent priest launched into the preparatory prayer with the steadiness and calm of old-school Blues singers.

"Oh, most merciful Jesus, with a contrite heart and penitent spirit, I bow down in profound humility before Thy divine majesty. I adore Thee, I hope in Thee, I love Thee above all things. I am heartily sorry for having offended Thee, my Supreme and Only God. I resolve to amend my life, and although I am unworthy to obtain mercy, yet the sight of Thy cross, on which Thou didst die, inspires me with hope and consolation...."

By the time the priest came to the final "Amen" a holy hush had settled over his flock, envisioning as they were the Way of the Cross that was to follow. The sermon focused on the need for redemption, urging churchgoers to examine their inner lives and reflect upon the values for which Christ gave his life. These readings, from the books of John 19 and Luke 23, set the stage for the subsequent procession to the Stations of the Cross. One of the altar boys, spying a quick gesture from the priest indicating his thirst, approached the lectern with a crystal glass and a carafe of water. He poured a healthy portion of "water"—in fact, vodka required by the priest to "steady his nerves"—into the glass from which the priest took a hefty swallow.

The priest then broke the bread and conducted sacrament. At the offering that followed, he urged everyone to yet again examine their consciences and give generously to God, as He had been generous to them. As the choir launched into song the altar boys brought out the bags and started collecting the offertory, carefully working the pews until everyone had been reached, including those gathered outside. After the priest had blessed the offerings, they were taken into the vestry and deposited in a particular bag.

The Way of the Cross began at the first of the two stations within the church compound where Jesus was condemned to death. The priest intoned in a deep and solemn voice, "We adore Thee, Oh Christ, and we praise Thee"—to which the flock genuflected, "Because by Thy holy cross Thou hast redeemed the world!"

"Christ" was represented by a solemn young man in starched white robes. The carpenter, who had been assigned the task of preparing the cross, had chosen a weighty mahogany and cut sharp edges that would dig into Christ's shoulders as he dragged it through the streets of Jerusalem on his way to Calvary. First, however, the procession had to travel the busy Maai Mahiu Road, up into the hills to the old church. The traffic marshals waved their arms in an authoritative manner, ensuring that everyone marched in single file up the winding road, hewn out of the cliff by Italian prisoners of war decades before. Massive eighteen-wheelers bore down on them periodically in clouds of exhaust, rumbling on their way from Nairobi to Rironi and Narok. As for the motorists caught up in the mile-long snarl-up behind the flock, there was little they could do but lean on their steering wheels and wait for the solemn procession to reach Golgotha.

The church members initially assumed their destination to be the tiny chapel built into the scarp by the Italian prisoners—the smallest Catholic church in the world. But the priest, who was at the head of the procession, turned abruptly, following a narrow track that wound its way up the escarpment, a track that had been traditionally used by herders and charcoal burners. It was a steep climb, but the priest urged them on. "Think of Christ," he told them, "who suffered for your sins."

The track negotiated its way through the craggy acacia and euphorbia trees that clung to the steep slope, and ended in a wide clearing at the top of the scarp, where the herders brought their cattle to browse on the grey moor. It was a spectacular place, with the expansive azure sky above them, and the Rift Valley spreading out below like a painting on a canvas. They were on the edge of a cliff, with the whole world spread out at their feet.

The priest did not allow the flock to admire the scenery for long. Raising his voice in the thin mountain air he reminded them that they were in the Lord's presence, and that they had to remove their shoes and prostrate themselves, lest they be smitten down. It was here that Jesus—so weary he could barely stand—was to be stripped of his garments in readiness to be nailed to the cross. "Simon of Cyrene" emerged from the acacia thickets, dragging the heavy mahogany cross behind him.

"Fac ut ardeat cor meum...in amando Christum Deum..." the

priest passionately declaimed as he gestured for the flock to prostrate themselves at the foot of the cross, their foreheads in the sand. In this focal moment around which the institution of the Church was built he found himself slipping easily into the language in which he had mastered the scriptures. The remaining parishioners, emerging from the thickets, gazed upon the afflicted Christ, his head crowned in thorns, his face streaked with tomato paste, and they were so overcome with emotion that they fell to the ground without instruction.

"We are on Golgotha, in the presence of our Lord's torment," the priest continued. "Lose yourself in prayer and you will surely feel the Lord's presence in this holy place; and if you should feel your body shaking or hands moving on your back, do not be afraid. Keep your head down and pray for repentance, for you are in the presence of our Lord and the heavenly angels will deliver you of your sins, which will be driven into the wild swine that live in the valley."

The altar boy, observing the strain on the priest's face, poured him another glass of "water," which the holy functionary drained in one deep swallow, readying himself for the penultimate stage of the Passion of the Christ. "*Sancta Mater istud agas,*" he continued, his face a film of sweat, his voice quivering with a passionate dedication to his task. "*Crucifixi fige plagas...*" The faithful lay prostrate in neat rows, their heads buried in the moor, each lost in their own personal meditation with God.

When the first pilgrim at the head of the file—a prominent butcher who owned several shops in Rironi, Narok, and Naivasha, in addition to a number of other enterprises he wished the church to know nothing about—felt the hands of the angels moving deftly upon his body, he tensed and became very still; when he felt them dart into his pockets and coax his wallet out of his back pocket, he became alarmed. Raising his head to look upon God's angel, the butcher found himself face to face with the business end of a 9mm Luger. The gun, which had materialized from the priest's vestments, was held at a professional hip level. The butcher had once been a thief, too, during the "coffee boom" years in the 1970s, when he had made his money across the Uganda border before laundering the proceeds to fund a legitimate business. He still possessed an acute instinct for danger.

"*Tui nati vulnerati,*" chanted the priest as he loomed above the flock. "*Jam dignati pro me pati…*" His expression was taut and strained, the monocle glittering in his ashen face like a sapphire in the ocular cavity of a skull. From the corner of his eye, the butcher saw an altar boy holding an Uzi sub-machine gun, standing guard over the prostrate pilgrims. The butcher silently lowered his gaze to the shiny tips of the priest's patent leather shoes, and the fingers of the angel who straddled him resumed a delicate caress of his body, darting in and out of hidden crevices to retrieve unholy items and purge the butcher of his sins.

The entire operation lasted just about an hour; the angels meticulously frisked every pilgrim, relieving them of their wallets, purses, cellphones, watches, and jewelry. When the task was completed, the priest stepped back and signaled with a raised hand. A car engine revved from within the thickets, and a beige van emerged. The angels, moving backward toward the van, kept the churchgoers covered with their Uzis.

Before climbing into the van, the priest stopped by the dazed-looking Christ who rested against the propped-up cross in his undergarments, awaiting his fate. The priest removed his golden rosary and dropped to one knee.

"Remember me with this when you get there," he whispered softly, his gaze locked with Christ's. "And please say a prayer for me and my sins. I now understand why the crowd chose you over the thief. All of us secretly crave to see the blood of an innocent man shed. It is a dark yearning that we all harbor inside. Have mercy on our poor souls, for we mortals are weak. Until we meet again in that place yonder, fare thee well."

The priest kissed the rosary and wrapped it around Christ's bloodied right hand, looping the tiny crucifix through the crook of his thumb so that it rested in his palm. "*Quando corpus morietur. Fac ut animae donetur. Paradisi gloria. Amen.*" He rose, made the sign of the cross, and hurried over into the van, which soon after sped off down a cattle track with a jolting rattle.

That evening, in a cottage on the banks of Lake Naivasha, the gang shared a bottle of Famous Grouse as they watched the sun set over the flame-tinged lake.

"You abandoned your flock on Golgotha, Cherie?" a lad by name of Saidi asked. Saidi had long since shed the altar boy's garments for jeans and a T-shirt. The rest of the gang was similarly attired, save for their leader, who wore his usual Italian suit and silk shirt, open at the neck to expose his gold necklace.

Without his monocle, moustache, and grey wig—which

he had discarded to reveal a clean-shaven head—Cherie looked like an altogether different man. He might have been a Hollywood star on the evening of the Oscars. He took a long pull on his cigar and gave his men a crafty smile. "'Crucified' them is the word, I think," he said softly.

"You truly will burn in hell for this one, Cherie. You took it too far this time. Why, even I was starting to believe in all that Latino stuff you were mumbling!" Saidi exclaimed.

"You forget that I *am* a priest," Cherie returned quietly. "And you forget your own part in the drama. If that day of vengeance ever comes, you can be sure that you will be roasting right next to me in the leaping flames. I would have been baptizing lost swine like you, if it were not for the sins of the flesh." By "sins of the flesh," Cherie meant women and liquor, both of which had proved irresistible prior to his being ordained. These particular failings were not uncommon among boarding school boys who proceeded to the seminary immediately upon graduation.

As the imposters relaxed by Lake Naivasha, it seemed likely that the faithful at Nyambari Parish Catholic Church had discovered their real priest and altar boys gagged and tied hand and foot in the vestry. The real panic, however, would doubtless come the following morning when the church members went to the bank. The gang's accomplice and IT consultant was at that very moment busy cleaning out the bank accounts of those whose ATM and ID cards had been pilfered by angelic hands—over two hundred in all. Apparently the gang had stumbled onto a goldmine with the wealth these churchgoers had kept hidden from God. If they had freely given ten percent of their wealth as prescribed by the

Bible, the Catholics could have built a new church in a new parish every week!

When the shit eventually hit the fan, it was the same IT specialist who would be called in by flustered bank managers to help fix the mess he had created—and get paid for it. And his was the work of a genius where it was difficult to tell where the lie ended and reality began. For when the butcher, among others, checked his monthly bank statement—which would be unusually long—he would find the December purchase of a truckload of sheep from the nearby Bidii Farm in his Rironi neighbourhood. The puzzle is that he had indeed bought sheep from this farmer in December, but only two in number rather than the truckload that amounted to thirty or more.

The IT technician, and talented architect of the electronic scam, was the only one who could disentangle the fine mess he had created in a multitude of client accounts. After several days of strenuous labor attempting to rectify the inexplicable accounting disaster, he would join his accomplices on a well-deserved holiday in Malindi as they planned their next big heist.

MERCEDES

Mugure sat at the counter of her *simu ya jamii*[70] booth and watched the street. With the cost of mobile phones falling and cell ownership on the rise, fewer people relied upon the community phone to make their calls. To make matters worse, the *simu ya jamii* was no longer the novelty investment concept in the low-income market that it had been in years past. Every one with a little cash to spare had rushed to open their own community phone booth, and now they dotted the street corners like mushrooms on a moist dung heap. Customers were few and far between, the competition cut-throat. These early investors were now grumbling that they should have invested in a *sukuma-wiki* kiosk instead, which consistently fetched considerably higher revenue—people had to eat, after all.

Perhaps it had not been such a bright idea after all, Mugure acknowledged, uncomfortably conscious of the fact that the booth had been her idea. When her stone-mason husband, Gichamba, had suggested she occupy herself with some line of business while he was away at the quarry, the phone business had immediately come to mind. Mugure's friend and neighbor, who ran her own *simu ya jamii* at the local market, made two hundred shillings on a bad day. At least that was what she had confided to Mugure.

Now, however, they were committed to the business. Con-

---

[70] community/public phone

struction work had been hard to find lately, and Gichamba's casual jobs at the quarry would not produce enough capital to start another business anytime soon. As Mugure contemplated her future with Gichamba her eyes strayed from the stream of villagers making their way along the dusty path to the glossy promotional poster pasted on her booth by the company that provided the mobile phone service. An E-Class brand-new Mercedes Benz leapt out of the poster amid thick wads of cash—the phone company's latest promotional prize to be given to one lucky recipient who submitted the winning SMS. A thin smile played upon Magure's lips. How could someone give away all that money? she wondered. They must be mad. Millions of shillings in prize money just for sending a simple text message? Perhaps it was some sort of scam, she mused. She had heard of countless cases where con artists had used mobile phones to defraud people, often netting millions.

Mugure, grappling with her own financial woes, could not help but wonder what she would do with all those millions if they were to come her way; daydreaming, after all, was free of charge. Just what *would* she do with all that money? *Ngai!* All those millions just for sending an SMS worth ten shillings....

The thought refused to leave her mind, and toward midday, feeling bored and drowsy—hardly anyone had come along to buy a scratch card or make a phone call—she reached for the phone to check how many call units remained on her account. There wasn't much money left in their account, and shaving ten shillings off would sink them even deeper in the red. But despite these thoughts, Mugure lowered her finger to the keyboard and started typing the text message.

A month had passed, and Mugure had long forgotten about the competition. The green poster, with the silver Mercedes leaping out of a wad of cash, had collected dust and curled and peeled off the kiosk wall in the stifling heat. The phone call came on a hot and drowsy afternoon, the heat just as oppressive as it had been on the day she'd first sent the text message, and her mood just as disgruntled. She had not had a single customer and was about to depart for a nearby food kiosk to buy some *githeri*[71] on credit.

"We are calling to inform you that the final draw of our recent retailers' promotion has just been concluded, and that we now have the winner of our grand prize. We would like you to confirm to us…"

Mugure gazed, bewildered, at the phone for a time, wondering if the caller had mistaken her for someone else. *This is a joke, and a cruel one at that*, she thought.

"Hello…hello…are you still there?" The voice had a tinny, unreal quality, when heard through the phone's cheap speaker, but there was no doubting what the man had said. Her finger descended, and without a second thought, she pressed the tiny red button, cutting off the persistent caller.

Mugure remained immobile for a while, her lunch forgotten, her breath hissing, her gaze unseeing. Still, in the depths of her mind, the caller's voice buzzed in her head like a fly hurling itself against a closed window pane. *A hoax*—the word played over and over in her mind as the silky smooth

---

[71] A meal of green maize and beans boiled together in a pot; popular in low-end city eateries because it is very cheap.

voice of the caller replayed in her mind like a stuck audio track. She had received phony text messages like this before, informing her she was the lucky winner of half-a-million shillings in some phone promotion or another. These messages were typically followed by a request for the lucky winner to send the small sum of money—a hundred shillings or so—by mobile phone money transfer in order to "facilitate the processing of the big cheque." This insignificant sum was from just one of the gullible millions who had fallen for the trick, their hundred bob contributing to a multi-million kitty. Some said that these scams were hatched at Kamiti Maximum Prison by canny convicts, who used the same mobile phone service to collect the money. Well, she would be daft to fall for it. Still, her pulse raced with every passing second, her thoughts a whirl, the voice of the caller still echoing in her mind. "We are calling to inform you…"

Mugure tore her gaze away from the dusty road and looked down at the cheap phone that was the source of her turmoil. And as if on cue the little LCD screen lit up and the handset started trilling. *Prrrrrrr!…prrrrrrrr!…prrrrrrrr!* The ring tone was crisp and piercing, refusing to be ignored. It unnerved her. She flipped open the dog-eared exercise book in which she had logged the four calls of the morning, bringing in fifty-two shillings—dented, stained coins that had undoubtedly spent time in a poker game or tossed around in a beggar's bowl. She fingered them idly, her thoughts whirring. *Prrrrr-rrrr!…prrrrrrrrr!*

Mugure closed the book, then jabbed the red button on her phone, pressing it firmly until the phone shut down. A long sigh escaped her lips after the electronic gadget finally stilled; the sudden silence felt oppressive, as if a felled giant tree had crashed through the branches and settled on the forest floor. She wiped her moist cheeks with the corner of her *khanga*, her eyes fixed to the dusty road but registering little of the human and donkey traffic. The little crowd of passersby seemed strangely detached, as did the traders in neighboring kiosks. Mechanically, Mugure went through the motions of closing shop, pushing the telescopic antenna down and swinging it until it clipped in place. Coiling the wire from the mouthpiece around the phone, she returned it to its box. She gathered the stack of unsold scratch cards and the meager coins from the day's trade and dropped them into the plastic container that had once contained washing detergent. Placing the container in her bag, she made her way slowly down the dusty road. It was almost midday and her shadow took the form of a stodgy pumpkin at her feet. A few people called a greeting as she made her way home, but she paid no heed.

When Gichamba returned home later that evening he found Mugure lying on her back on their narrow bed, staring up at the rafters, her kiosk bag on the table.

"Mugure," he called. "Are you all right?"

Typically, Mugure would remain at the phone kiosk until evening, seeking to capitalize on late workers returning home. After Gichamba had taken his bath, he would replace her at the kiosk while she went home to prepare supper.

The first thought that came to his mind was one that came naturally to a newly married young man. His gaze lingered upon the curve of her breast, provocatively pointed beneath her white nylon blouse, and the flat expanse of her belly beneath her tightly wrapped *khanga*.

Mugure turned her head slightly and her eyes found his. "Is that you, Gichamba?" she asked. Their single-roomed timber shack was dimly lit by a small window, and Gichamba could see only the outlines of their scant furniture—two stools, a rickety table hammered out of dismantled tomato crates, a cheap Chinese stove, and the bed, fashioned of gunnysacks and straw, upon which his new wife lay.

"It is I, my dear," he said, approaching Mugure. "What is the matter? Why aren't you at the kiosk? It is not the Town Council people again, is it?" he asked in a whisper. "They didn't...?"

"No," Mugure replied softly. "The kiosk is still standing. Nothing is the matter, Gichamba."

"Is there a problem with the phone handset?" he murmured fearfully, almost more to himself than his wife. He hadn't yet completed payment for the phone, which he had acquired on credit from a friend at the shopping center. With shaking hands, Gichamba retrieved the phone from Mugure's bag and pressed the green button. As the strength of the phone's signal stabilized the beep-beep of recorded messages sounded, the flashing icon an eerie firefly glow in the dark room. Glancing over at his wife, who remained prone upon the bed, Gichamba was startled by the sudden ringing of the phone. *Prrrrrr! ...prrrrrrr! ...prrrrrrrrr!*

"Go on, answer it," Mugure urged.

Gichamba looked at her for a while, confused at her manner. The phone kept on ringing, the caller at the other end insistent. Gichamba gingerly lifted the receiver to his ear, wiping the moisture from his face with the back of his left hand.

"H-hello," he stammered.

"Good evening," a smooth voice replied. "I've been trying to reach a lady I spoke with earlier today on this number. Is she available, please?"

"That lady is my wife—" Gichamba began.

"And what is her name, please?" the caller interjected, as if afraid Gichamba might hang up.

"Her name is Mugure," said Gichamba. "Trizah Mugure." He was about to add 'Gichamba' but decided it might not be important.

"And how old is she, please?"

Gichamba scratched his head. Was she twenty or twenty-one? "I'll have to ask her. May I know why you want to speak to her?"

"I have news for her that will change her life, news that she cannot afford to miss. I am sure she will soon share it with you. Please ask her to take the phone."

Gichamba, his mind racing, cupped his hand over the mouthpiece and signaled his wife with his index finger. Mugure reluctantly swung her legs over the side of the bed and rose with a sigh. Gichamba gave her the phone, then reached into his pocket for a cigarette stub he had saved from an earlier smoke. His hands were trembling suddenly with nervousness.

"Yes," Mugure said softly into the mouthpiece.

Gichamba retrieved a match and lit the tin lamp on the table, its wavering light illuminating Mugure's round cheeks and the gleam of her eyes. Cupping the still-lit match, he raised it to the cigarette stub in his mouth, sucking in one end to ignite the damp wrapping.

"Yes..." Mugure repeated into the mouthpiece, then paused a moment before her hand flew to her chest and she let out a loud gasp, her eyes wide.

"What is it?" asked Gichamba, alarmed. "What does he say?"

For answer Mugure held out the handset. "Speak to him," she said, her voice a hoarse croak.

"Hello," Gichamba muttered, his hand trembling. "Yes... yes...you mean—?" His mouth dropped open and his cigarette stub fell unnoticed to the ground.

After the caller had hung up, Gichamba and Mugure sat at the table for some time, the flickering lamp throwing long grotesque shadows around them. The night breeze whistled in through the open window, and a swarm of mosquitoes and other night insects gathered around the naked flame. At length Gichamba rose and closed the window. Then he came back and settled on one of the stools across from his wife.

"Mugure, is it true?" he asked at last.

"You heard him," said Mugure softly.

"It is not some sort of a mistake? I...I mean, you took part in this competition, didn't you?" Mugure nodded, her eyes locked on her husband's. "A car, is that what the man said?" said Gichamba, disbelieving.

"Not a car, Gichamba. A *Mercedes*," Mugure corrected him.

"*Ngai!*" Gichamba muttered softly. "*Ngai!*"

From the neighbouring shacks they could hear the sounds of their neighbours finishing up their evening meals and preparing to retire. Mugure had intended to buy two cups of *githeri* from the woman who cooked the beans and maize mixture down the block and cook it together with some potatoes and cabbage for their supper, but the phone call had interrupted their evening plans.

"Are you hungry?" she asked her husband.

"No. What about you?" he replied. Mugure shook her head, her eyes staring vacantly into the semi-darkness. "Let's go to bed," he said, rising to his feet.

They stacked the phone equipment carefully under the bed and blew out the lamp. As Gichamba and Mugure undressed and crawled under the thin blanket they shared they both knew it was going to be a long, sleepless night.

A scrawny rooster, who lived in a neighbor's outhouse, shattered the pre-dawn stillness promptly at five a.m. every morning with an ear-splitting squawk. As the bird flapped its wings into a flurry, warming up its throat for another exertion, the creak of wooden doors announced their disheveled, half-dressed neighbor. He routinely hosed the untidy kei apple hedge that lined their block of shacks with steaming urine, to the accompaniment of muffled farts. Then, on cue, padded footfalls were heard on the path as the early laborers made their way to the workplaces where they had hawked their services the day before, trying their luck for a daily wage.

It had been a long night of sleepless vigil for Gichamba. In the small hours his eyes had finally closed, but it was the fleeting sleep of the weary that leaves just as quickly as it arrives. He lit the tin lamp and went to wash his face in a plastic washbasin by the door, drawing cold water from one of the two jerry cans in which they stored their daily ration, obtained from the communal tap outside the landlord's house. As Gichamba cleaned his teeth with his herbal chew-stick, Mugure rose from their bed.

The strange silence of the night before persisted as they silently ate their simple breakfast of freshly baked *mandazi,* purchased from the roadside seller and washed down with black tea.

"What shall we wear?" Mugure asked at last, after she had cleared the table.

"I don't know. Just put on anything you feel comfortable in," Gichamba replied.

"I wonder if I should borrow a dress. Do you think they'll want us to pose for photos?"

"Certainly," Gichamba affirmed. "I think the newspaper people will want a picture to put in the newspapers."

"You think newspaper people will come?" Mugure asked warily. "I mean, we are not that important...?"

"There is no doubt about that. They will be there, trust me. A prize like this must be covered."

"And what will *you* wear?" Mugure asked, reaching above the bed to retrieve several wire hangers—upon which her finest dresses hung—from nails in the rafters. She had carefully washed the dresses, pressed them with a coal iron borrowed from a neighbour, and stowed them inside long brown launderer's bags to keep them free of smoke and dust.

"Oh, I'm fine just the way I am," Gichamba said, smoothing down his faded denim jacket and creased brown corduroys.

"But those are your work clothes, Gichamba," Mugure protested, disapprovingly. "I think you should find something more decent for the photos. Perhaps you should persuade your friend Ndirangu to lend you his new shirt, the white checked one that he wore on Sunday when you went out to the shopping centre."

"I say, you are creating a fuss about nothing, Mugure," Gichamba said. "In any case, I don't suppose I'll be required to pose beside you."

Mugure stripped down to her petticoat and tried on one of the dresses, smoothing it down carefully and turning to look back over her shoulder, as if she were wearing it for the first time. "It's too tight around the hips, don't you think, Gichamba?" she asked.

"Oh, it looks just fine to me," Gichamba said, settling on one of the stools and lighting a cigarette stub that he had saved from the previous day.

Dissatisfied with the fit of the old dress, Mugure shrugged out of it and tried on the other.

"Shouldn't we find someone to accompany us?" she asked as she smoothed down the faded chiffon print dress she had bought at the local *mutumba* market. "Perhaps Aunt Muthoni could meet us in town? And if we have to conduct interviews with newspaper people, Aunt Muthoni would know what to say."

"If you say so," Gichamba said with a shrug. "It is your car, anyway," he added with a nervous laugh. His nearest relation was miles away in Molo; it would take a day's travel to get here, and another to raise the money for bus fare.

"It is *our* car, remember," Mugure said, adjusting the hook and eye at the back of the dress collar.

"Yes, our car. Sorry," Gichamba said, taking a long drag at

the diminishing cigarette stub.

Mugure fussed over her hair, working a stove-heated comb through her locks. The comb sizzled with each pull through her greased hair, emitting a pungent aroma of burnt tripe.

"Hurry up with that, will you?" he said impatiently, rising to his feet. "We should be on our way by now. Didn't the man say half past eight?"

"I'm almost done," Mugure said, peering into a cracked shard of mirror.

Gichamba glanced at his cheap quartz watch. "I say, you'll find me at the bus stop," he called over his shoulder as he ducked through the door and ambled across their stony yard. At the bus stop several town-bound *matatus* stopped and sped away before Mugure finally came hurrying up the path. She stopped to brush the fine red dust from her calves, kicked up by her plastic sandals and stuck to the generous smear of Vaseline Mugure had applied to her legs.

"What took you so long?" Gichamba muttered irritably.

"I had to make the phone call first, or had you forgotten?"

"And did you talk to your aunt? What did she say?"

Muthoni, Mugure's aunt, disliked Gichamba, and Gichamba disliked her. Mugure had moved in with Gichamba six months before, and Aunt Muthoni had made her displeasure at the arrangement very clear. Despite the fact that she had never been properly married herself, she never refrained from dropping annoying hints that Gichamba should hurry along his traditional arrangements for acquiring a wife.

"Ow, you don't know half how excited Aunt Muthoni was when I broke the news!" Mugure exclaimed. "Indeed, she insisted on joining us at the Ambassadeur bus stop so she could meet the prize people with us."

"Is it?" Gichamba acknowledged reluctantly. "Well, she'd better hurry. I don't think we have the time to wait for her. Did you remember to bring the phone?"

"It is right here," Mugure said, tapping her black bag. "How could I forget something like that? The man said we would need it as proof."

"Do you have your identification?"

"Yes," said Mugure, gesturing toward her bosom where she concealed her purse in the cup of her bra.

"All right. Let's get on our way then."

At that moment a *matatu* swept round the bend, the driver signaling with the horn and flashing headlights when he spied them waiting. Gichamba flagged the *matatu* down and they squeezed in, Mugure taking the only vacant seat and her husband standing on the running board beside the conductor.

Aunt Muthoni spotted them from the crowded Ambassadeur stage, hailing them with a shout and a frantically waving arm. She was dressed in an expensive *kitenge*[72] dress, of a West African pattern and cut that Gichamba had never seen before, her hair tucked behind an elaborate headdress of the same fabric. Her attire was accentuated by white patent leather pumps and a matching handbag clutched under her arm. With her was another middle-aged woman—another aunt, Gichamba later learned—who sported an equally elaborate coiffure and dress. Gichamba and Mugure, fighting against the jostling tide of early office workers, who leapt off buses

---

[72] A print cotton fabric with a garish African design common in tropical Africa.

in a hurry to get to their stations ahead of the boss, made their way over to the aunts who impatiently awaited them. As Mugure was engulfed in hugs reeking of designer perfume, Gichamba could only wonder how the aunts had managed to get from Wangige to town on such short notice and in such splendid attire.

"Oh, and how are you today, Gichamba?" Aunt Muthoni finally acknowledged his presence, offering him her slim hand.

"I am fine, thank you," said Gichamba, taking her hand. Her hand slipped in and out of his in a flash, barely completing the gesture, cold as a fish.

"I'm hungry. Let's find somewhere to have a cup of tea," Aunt Muthoni stated, shepherding them across the street, her arm draped protectively across Mugure's shoulder. "Besides, we need to find a place to sit so that we can plan this great event ahead of us. God knows, we need to celebrate this good fortune that has visited Mugure, don't you all agree?"

Gichamba had little choice but to follow, his unpolished mine boy's boots scraping along on the chipped pavement like a reluctant dog on a leash. Twice he had to strike himself a discreet blow to the head, reminding himself to remain cheerful despite the wave of pessimism suddenly flooding through him.

Following behind the expensively clad aunts, he wondered what kind of restaurant they had in mind. After the bus fare home he had only a hundred shillings to his name. A cold sweat broke out upon his brow.

Breakfast turned out to be at a fancy restaurant on the corner—just as he had feared—and consisted of several courses. Their uniformed waiter brought a tiny bowl of soup, meant to whet their appetites before the main course. Aunt Muthoni had ordered for them all, saving everyone the trouble of trying to decipher exotic culinary terms like soufflé and omelet. Gichamba was perplexed by the array of silverware laid out like a surgeon's tools, wondering why so many knives and spoons were required for a simple meal like tea.

"This is where the people of *your* class eat, my dear Mugure," Aunt Muthoni announced primly as she adjusted Mugure's napkin in her lap and provided her with a soup spoon. Gichamba she left to sweat it out on his own. "This is how people who drive a Mercedes live, my dear," she added with a generous laugh, the fat rolls under her chin quivering merrily. Aunt Muthoni gestured toward the plush, wall-length brocade curtains and the crystal chandelier that was suspended from the roof. Then, nodding her satisfaction, she shook out a rose-tinted napkin and dabbed daintily at the lipstick that smudged the corners of her mouth.

"You are right," Aunt Wanjiru chimed in. "Mugure, you are so lucky to have an aunt who knows these things. This kind of knowledge will be useful when you have to have dinner with the company directors at the prize-giving ceremony."

Mugure nodded, nervously, discreetly wiping at the soup she had spilled on her dress.

The hot breakfast consisted of a barely cooked egg, a sausage, and razor-thin slices of mutton; the tea required a manipulation of all manner of tiny steel pots, and the butter, bread, and sauces arrived in anonymous foil-wrapped portions, one indistinguishable from the other. Aunt Muthoni and her friend smiled at the fussy waiters, as if they breakfasted at the Hilton daily. Indeed, Gichamba mused, it was hard to recognize the two women, who even yesterday drank millet porridge from chipped enamel mugs as they haggled with barefoot village women at a cabbage and *waru*[73] stall in Wangige market.

The bill arrived ceremoniously, tucked inside a leather folder that rested on a gleaming white saucer. Gichamba coughed slightly and reached for a toothpick, busying himself trying to extract an imaginary morsel stuck between his teeth.

Aunt Muthoni casually reached over to retrieve the folder, glancing inside before folding it shut. She signaled the hovering waiter with a wave of her hand as she reached into her Gucci handbag with the other. Fishing a blood-red wallet from the depths of her handbag, Aunt Muthoni flicked it open sufficiently wide so they could all see the credit cards and travelers cheques stacked within. Just as casually, she peeled out a bunch of thousands, which she slipped into the folder beside the bill and pushed toward the waiter. The waiter, in his turn, bowed deeply and disappeared with the saucer. Gichamba, stunned, thought it the most blatant display of wealth that he had ever encountered.

Belching deeply, Aunt Muthoni rose and smoothed her dress. "I think we are ready to go," she announced, picking up her handbag. "Next stop is a boutique where we'll get Mugure dressed up properly. She has to look good in front of the cameras, you know."

---

[73] Irish potatoes

Gichamba rose to his feet, certain that there was very little role, if any, for him in this tightly woven script. He felt like the shabby gardener who had been dragged to his master's staff party, well aware that the wielder of the purse strings held the true position of power.

As Mugure stood to leave, a phone began to ring. *Prrrrrr-rr...prrrrrrrr...prrrrrrrrrr!*

Aunt Muthoni froze, her carefully cultivated composure momentarily jarred by the shrill sound. "Would that be my phone?" she asked, a furrow of lines appearing on her heavily made-up brow as she reached into her handbag and pulled out a slick titanium-cased phone. It quickly became apparent, however, that the shrill ringing came from the shabby black bag on the floor by Mugure's feet.

The aunts and Gichamba again took their seats and waited as Mugure removed the various bulky parts of the phone from the bag and assembled them on the table. There was, however, a critical component missing—a charging unit fashioned out of an old car battery, a chunky hand-crafted adaptor, and discarded crocodile clips that a local mechanic had fabricated. Too bulky to fit in a bag, the charger was used only at home. Fortunately, the phone was sufficiently charged for Mugure, with trembling hands, to make a call.

Aunt Muthoni drew her seat closer to her niece, straining to follow the conversation. The phone company wanted to send a vehicle to fetch them. A silver-capped ballpoint pen appeared in Aunt Muthoni's hand as if by magic, and she quickly scribbled the name of the restaurant and the street on a napkin, pushing it toward the perspiring Mugure. The caller confirmed the address and informed them that a company vehicle would be coming shortly to fetch them.

Mugure was a bundle of nerves as they waited outside, suddenly conscious of her cheap plastic sandals and dusty, cracked feet, and thinking wistfully of the boutique they no longer had time to visit. Aunt Muthoni rubbed Mugure's shoulder in an attempt to put her at ease. A few minutes later, a green van bearing the logo of the phone company appeared round the bend, cruising slowly down the street. The vehicle stopped beside the restaurant and the passenger door opened to reveal a beefy man in a suit and tie. Stepping onto the pavement, he hesitantly approached the group.

"*Habari!*[4] I am looking for a young woman by the name of Mugure …Trizah Mugure," he said.

"Good morning, sir," Aunt Muthoni cried, flashing a million-dollar smile. "This here is Mugure, and I am her aunt, Muthoni. Are you from the phone company?"

"Yes, that's right, madam," said the company official with a wide smile. "And I guess you know already the good news I bring to your niece! But perhaps the sidewalk is not the best place to break the news, yes?" he added, his attention shifting smoothly from Muthoni to Mugure. "Perhaps we can get in the car and find somewhere better?"

The company official shepherded the bewildered Mugure into the back of the van and seated himself next to her, fussing over her like a favourite uncle. From a cool-box, he produced chilled bottles of mineral water and passed them around. Deprived of her charge, Aunt Muthoni climbed into the passenger seat beside the driver, her expensive handbag clasped in her lap. After settling herself, she called a friend

---

[4] Swahili for 'greetings'

on her titanium-cased phone, chattering away in a mix of English, Swahili, and Gikuyu, loudly enough so that all could hear the details of the lucrative business deal she was negotiating. Gichamba slid the door of the air-conditioned van shut as the driver engaged the gear shift, and they rolled away into Nairobi City's bumper-to-bumper traffic.

Gichamba blew out the tin lamp and lay wearily upon his bed. It was past midnight, and he could hear his neighbours snoring through the thin wooden walls. He had stopped by a kiosk on his way home and bought a packet of cigarettes, which had kept him company through the long, restless night. He wished Mugure were with him. They had agreed, however, that Mugure should be based at Aunt Muthoni's house in Wangige for the time being. The phone company staff could collect and return her without concern for their own relatively run-down shack or lack of security. While it would take three days of paperwork and publicity photos before they took possession of the car, Gichamba and Mugure had now joined the prestigious class of people who owned a factory-fresh Mercedes Kompressor.

Gichamba still could not believe it. They had had the opportunity to sit in the Mercedes earlier that day, and he could still smell the leather upholstery, feel the sleek curve of the silver hood, and recall his admiration of the three-pointed star mounted on the bonnet. He had felt an almost electrical charge, sitting behind the wheel and inserting the key fob in the ignition, knowing that he was at the wheel of one of the most impressive vehicles ever to travel the roads. The staff seemed to realize that neither Gichamba, Mugure, nor Aunt

Muthoni knew how to drive because they smoothly guided them through the procedure of opening and starting an automatic Mercedes. The staff had patiently explained the intricacies of the car's computers and the other automated complexities that kept that icon of class on the road. Mugure had been too nervous to sit in the driver's seat, and despite Aunt Muthoni's offer to tutor her, the company officials requested Gichamba take the wheel. Even in the excitement of the moment, the power play taking place in the wings was not lost on Gichamba.

The flurry of activities that had followed left his head in a spin. News people, hungry for a front-page piece, swarmed over them like vultures to a fresh carcass, camera bulbs flashing, shouting countless stupid questions like, "Do you have a bank account?" or, "Was that your first time inside a Mercedes?" Salespeople in grey suits lurked in the crowd like jackals at a lion's kill, seeking a moment alone with the lucky winner so that they could cut a deal. All manner of banking types waited to seize the winners' attentions, keen to offer investment advice should the couple decide to sell the car. Among these were the curious onlookers, awed at the notion of giving away a Mercedes Kompressor to a couple of cracked-heeled peasants who could not tell satnav from central locking. At last the company staff muscled them out of the crowd for lunch, Aunt Muthoni and her accomplice marshaling Mugure along like her twin shadows, with Gichamba left to play catch-up, lugging the black elections observer's bag with the chunky phone equipment inside. He'd barely had the chance to hand Mugure the black bag and slip her his hundred shillings before she was whisked away in a taxi.

Now, as he reflected on the events of the day it occurred to him that their lives had taken a dramatic twist. They were no longer ordinary laborers trying to scrape together a living on the brinks of the mean and sprawling city. Now they were in the money and could afford to live "the high life."

The following morning, Gichamba left their shack to retrieve a newspaper. As he had feared Mugure's face was splashed across the front of both the *Nation* and the *Standard*. POOR GIRL WINS AN E-CLASS MERCEDES, one headline proclaimed. TO BED A PAUPER, RISE A MILLIONAIRE read another. The papers depicted a photo of Mugure perched gingerly on the bonnet, a shy smile curling the corner of her cracked lips, one dusty foot in its cheap sun-bleached sandal swinging over the gleaming fender of the nine-million-shilling silver Mercedes.

Gichamba bought both papers, folded them carefully inside his jacket, and strolled to a nearby food kiosk where he would have a quiet place to read the articles. Seating himself at a quiet back table, he ordered tea and *mandazi* before reading through each article twice, memorizing every word as if he were a student preparing for an exam. He appeared in one photograph featured in the *Standard* article, a dim figure at the back of the crowd, clutching the black elections observer's bag that contained the magic phone. Aunt Muthoni appeared prominently in nearly all the pictures, standing proudly beside Mugure and flashing a bright smile at the cameras.

"I think I know that girl," said a waiter, who had noiselessly appeared at his elbow. "Isn't she the one who runs a phone kiosk down the road? *Ngai!* She won a Mercedes? She sold me a scratch card just the other day!"

Gichamba finished his tea in a hurry and left, his face trained on the dusty path, avoiding the gaze of people on the street. As he approached the wooden kiosk where his wife ran the phone business, he noticed a white car parked beside it. A woman in office attire leaned against the car bonnet, sipping coffee from a travel flask and chatting with a tall, thin man in faded jeans and a khaki windbreaker. Slung around the man's neck was a camera fitted with an expensive telescopic lens. Gichamba didn't need to be told who they were.

Without a second thought he turned on his heel, pretending to buy a cigarette at a kiosk across the street, all the while watching the journalists from the corner of his eye. They wanted to unearth every detail of the lives of the peasant couple who had hit the jackpot; to dig out the extent of their penury and lay it bare for the voyeuristic public as if they were a disemboweled carcass on a butcher's hook.

Gichamba hurried up the road to a market *muratina*[75] den where the owner sold the potent *chang'aa* liquor by the tot.

"*Karibu*, Gichamba," the elderly proprietor greeted him, flashing a gap-toothed smile as he hurried over with a dripping glass. "It is unusual to see you here at this hour."

Gichamba dug into his pocket and took out a handful of coins, counting out the money as the old man poured the drink and placed it on the table. The proprietor, however, refused payment. Leaning close, he whispered, his breath a blast of stale *mutura* and *chang'aa*: "This is on me, Gichamba.

---

[75] A traditional Kikuyu alcoholic drink distilled from wild honey and herbs.

It is for the car. We are all so proud!"

Apparently, Gichamba learned, the story had been featured on the previous evening's seven o'clock news, and watched by crowds of people on the cheap Greatwall TVs installed in the social places around the market.

"Gichamba, you really have made this village proud," the old man said with a wink, still grinning broadly. "I never imagined that one of our own would be on TV some day!"

Gichamba raised the glass and took a long swig, the ammoniac fumes biting the back of his nostrils. He gulped hungrily, welcoming the sting of the harsh liquor as it spread like molten lava in the pit of his stomach. He was clearly going to get drunk early today.

❧

Mugure, similarly, was trying to come to terms with the transformation wrought in the past twelve hours. The massive bed in Aunt Muthoni's house, with its down-feathered coverlet and pristine white sheets, felt strange after her straw-stuffed gunnysack mattress. Worried that she was somehow soiling the sheets, and lacking the familiar sound of roaches scavenging for scraps, Mugure slept poorly. Upon waking, she was confronted by such an array of breakfast delicacies she had been spoilt for choice.

Several beauticians hired by Aunt Muthoni for what was, no doubt, a princely sum were now intent upon transforming her from a backwoods peasant to a fashionable young lady of the city. They had coaxed her wiry hair into a chick bob, applied all manner of gels and potions to her face, neck, and upper body, and were now employed in lavishing polish on her fingernails and toenails. It was a lengthy process, but they were doing their best to keep Mugure entertained. One attendant gently massaged her shoulders in the adjustable ergonomic chair, with its foot and head rest and rotating massage beads. A stack of glossy fashion magazines and chilled, freshly pressed fruit juice was situated carefully within reach.

This, Mugure thought, must surely be the lap of luxury, and yet in the back of her mind she felt unsettled. She hadn't talked to her husband in over twelve hours, and she had started to worry about him. She wondered if her parents in Kerugoya had heard the news, perhaps from one of the wealthier villagers who owned a TV set or the headmaster of the village school who habitually bought a newspaper. Mugure would have liked to have called them, but her parents— like their neighbors, small-scale farmers necessarily focused on scratching out a meagre subsistence from tiny patches of land—didn't own a phone.

As the beauticians gently immersed Mugure's feet in a milk solution to soften chapped and roughened skin in readiness for a cosmetic peel, Aunt Muthoni breezed into the yard wearing a burgundy terrycloth robe with a Marriot logo on the breast, her hair wrapped in a thick rose-colored towel.

"And how's our little queen today?" she asked, smiling brightly.

"I am fine, Aunt Muthoni," Mugure replied with a demure smile.

"Really?" Aunt Muthoni looked her niece up and down with a critically appraising air. "I can see we are finally getting somewhere with you," she said with satisfaction. "Now you are starting to look like a real lady. I will leave you in the capable hands of these lovely girls for now as I make some phone calls. Just let the maid know when you are done, girls, won't you?" With that, Aunt Muthoni sauntered off, her ample hips swinging in the robe, a tune humming on her lips.

The car that Mugure had won was sold the following day, with the dealer who handled the sale knocking three-quarters of a million off the showroom price before deducting his own commission. "Remember this is a Mercedes. And one thing you should know about a Mercedes is that it starts to depreciate in value the moment you turn on the ignition," he advised his clients. "Why, in some cases, the car will lose value the moment it leaves the showroom, regardless of whether it was even turned on or not!"

The same afternoon the car was sold, Mugure's parents arrived from Kerugoya. Wanjiru, it turned out, had been dispatched in a taxi earlier to fetch them after Aunt Muthoni had noted Mugure's growing anxiety.

"Mugure, is that really you?" Mugure's mother exclaimed as she stepped out of the cab, her stained teeth flashing in a radiant smile. "Is this really my Mugure?"

Mugure's mother was a small woman clad in her country Sunday best—a thick hand-knitted brown jersey, worn over a faded nylon dress that fell to her ankles. Her thick, corny toes poked through holes in her tattered canvas shoes, and tufts of grey hair sprouted from beneath her tightly tied head cloth. She embraced her daughter, her callused farm-toughened hands mussing the elaborate bob as she fussed over Mugure, both women with tears in their eyes.

Mugure's father clambered out of the car, yanking up the band of his oversized tweed trousers and adjusting the frayed coat that nearly swallowed his bony frame. Slapping a worn fedora on his bald pate, he approached his daughter, his dark eyes assessing her with the same scrutiny he applied to the cattle he traded at the Saturday village market.

"Baba," Mugure said, shaking her father's bony hand.

"How are you, my daughter?" His wizened face split into a huge smile, and the grey stubble in the folds of his chin quivered as he shook with laughter. "Mugure, is this really you?" His bout of mirth ended in a prolonged wheezy cough. The old man spat a fat wad of tobacco-stained phlegm into the dust and rubbed it in with the heel of his worn *akala* shoe.

After bathing, Mugure's parents were to be driven to town to be outfitted in new clothes and shoes, after which the old man would be deposited at a bar in the Wangige market. Aunt Muthoni had carefully selected this particular bar because of the band's *mugithi*[76] songs and the elderly clientele the music attracted. The taxi driver, under strict instructions to ensure that the old man lacked for nothing, would bring him home after the evening's festivities were over.

The women, meanwhile, retired to the backyard to catch up on the latest news from the village, carrying a pot of strongly brewed tea and soft-boiled *ngwaci*.[77]

Mugure's elderly parents rested in cane chairs on the verandah, a glass of fresh fruit juice at the old woman's elbow, and a bottle of cold Tusker at her husband's. His crisp new shirt was unbuttoned at the collar and a new Stetson rested in his lap. Between two thick, calloused fingers, he held

---

[76] A music style of the Kikuyu people that borrows from the colonial English waltzes and church music rhythms.

[77] sweet potatoes

a hand-rolled cigarette—the kind that make women pinch their noses—and periodically flicked the ash into the carpet, forgetting the heavy cut-glass ashtray that sat on the table. Aunt Muthoni had tried to coax Mugure's father into smoking the more fashionable Sportsmans cigarettes instead of this foul-smelling variety, but he was not to be persuaded. There was something about taking a pinch of shag out of his worn leather pouch, spreading it on a scrap of old newspaper and adding a touch of spittle as he worked it with his fingers that was akin to a ritual.

An insistent rattle of iron and chain sounded from the driveway below. "Is there a visitor at the gate?" Mugure's father asked, craning his neck to look over the veranda.

"Yes," his wife confirmed, leaning over the railing. "A man."

Although situated in the outskirts of the city, Wangige was not a particularly safe place to live. Aunt Muthoni, like other wealthy residents, had walled herself in behind chain-link fences and a six-foot-high wrought-iron gate. Wangige could not be more unlike his idyllic home town of Kerugoya, the old man reflected, where he could take a shortcut through a neighbor's farm and catch the family at their midday meal in the shade of a banana grove.

Gichamba walked stiffly up the short drive behind the maid, his boots crunching on the gravel, conscious of the scrutiny of the elderly couple from the veranda. He had barely slept, had little appetite, and was miserable at the lack of communication with Mugure. He had tried calling the number of the phone in the black elections observer's bag from a payphone, but he had been consistently greeted by the recorded message: "the subscriber cannot be reached."

Muthoni had orchestrated this separation, he knew with bitter conviction. She intended to oversee the sale of the car, to manage the funds, to call the shots. But he might have something to say about that, Gichamba thought grimly. But despite Muthoni's machinations, why hadn't Mugure made an effort to communicate?

Ndirangu, his friend and fellow quarry worker, had urged Gichamba to find his wife and confront her aunt at their house in Wangige, which Gichamba had decided to do. He had not realized, however, that Mugure's parents were also visiting. While Gichamba had never visited Mugure's family home to formally ask for her hand, and had, in fact, never met her parents, the old woman on the veranda bore a striking resemblance to his wife.

"Habari, *Mzee*...habari, Mama," Gichamba greeted her as he stepped on to the veranda.

The old man eyed Gichamba steadily, wiping the ring of beer foam from his upper lip with the back of his hand. "You are the young man who lives with my daughter, aren't you?" he said gruffly.

"That's right, *Mzee*," Gichamba replied, ducking his head respectfully.

"So, now you have come to visit us?" he added as he stuck his rolled cigarette between his lips and began searching through his trouser pocket for an ancient tin lighter.

"Er...yes, *Mzee*," said Gichamba uncomfortably, extending his hand, offering a handshake, which Mugure's father ignored.

Gichamba, following the maid into the house, was shown

187

to a deep armchair by the door and left on his own. Perching on the edge of the chair, he felt conscious of the trail of dirt his boots had left on the thick sea-green carpet. A slight breeze, blowing through the open windows, caused the crystal chandelier to swing gently, sending a cascade of rainbow-colored light across the walls. A four-foot aquarium, filled with tiny goldfish that darted around giant seashells and exotic aquatic plants, dominated one corner of the room. How was it that a vegetable and egg trader could afford to live in such affluence? Gichamba wondered. Through an open door across the room, he could see a large mahogany table being set for lunch.

It was a tense meal, knives and spoons doing most of the talking as bowls of gravy passed quietly from hand to hand. Mugure's father, seated opposite Gichamba, carved the massive rack of roast goat ribs, pausing every so often to glare at the young man, conveying a message that only the two of them understood: *I am yet to eat your goat ribs, kijana.* Mugure had been seated between her mother and Aunt Muthoni, where it was difficult for Gichamba to make eye contact with her. The little conversation they had was strained, initiated by the old man and deftly guided by him such that often it ended on a cryptic phrase that only the best speakers of the language could interpret, but which nonetheless was laden with meaning.

At length, as everyone chewed their toothpicks to a pulp, Muthoni rose and asked Mugure to help her clear the table. One by one the women disappeared onto the kitchen until only Gichamba and the old man remained.

"That was a hearty meal," the old man said with a deep

belch. "And now, a little fresh air settles the belly. What do you say, *kijana?*"

The two men settled in the cane chairs on the verandah, just as the maid appeared with another cold Tusker for the old man and a beer for Gichamba.

"So, you came to visit us, you say?" the old man asked.

"Yes, I came to visit you, is true," Gichamba acknowledged, steadily returning his gaze. "I also came to fetch my wife and to determine what should be done about our car."

"Your *wife*, you say?" said the old man, a crafty look in his eyes.

"Yes, my wife," Gichamba affirmed, taking a sip of his beer.

"And would that be my daughter you are speaking of?"

"I believe we are talking about Mugure," Gichamba replied levelly.

"You will forgive my expression of surprise, young man. You see, I am hearing this for the first time," said the old man, licking at the edge of a square of old newspaper as he rolled up another cigarette. "Indeed I am hearing of this for the first time."

At that moment Aunt Muthoni and Mugure's mother bustled through the doors, settling themselves in the remaining cane chairs.

"*Nyina wa Mugure*,"[78] said the old man, making a half-hearted effort to rise from his chair. "It is good that you have come. This young man here was amusing me just now. It seems like some matters have been going on behind my

---

[78] Kikuyu for 'Mother to Mugure,' a formal way an elder might address his wife.

back, would that be so?"

"I do not understand, *Mzee*," said Mugure's mother. "Of what are you speaking?"

"It is truly amusing," said the old man, pausing to light his cigarette. "I come all this way to visit my daughters in the city and then, after being received so well I stumble on the information that one of them is married; and yet I have never tasted a horn-full of *muratina* in the marriage negotiations as the girl's father! What do you think of that, *Nyina wa Mugure*?" The old man's chest was heaving in a burst of wheezy laughter that caused tears to spring to his eyes. "I say, isn't that plain amusing, *Nyina wa Mugure*?" he repeated breathlessly, dabbing at his wet lips. "Or was this your plan, Muthoni, to invite me over and then pull this surprise on me?"

By the time Gichamba left two hours later the air was charged, brimming with such hostility it would catch fire if someone struck a match. The entire clan had come out on the veranda to confront Gichamba and their collective vehemence had finally driven the young man to the front door where Muthoni issued the parting shot.

"Look at him," Muthoni spat. "He has no shame at all, coming here, eating free food, and then having the audacity to ask for his wife…what wife do you have here, Gichamba?"

"You know very well what brought me here, Muthoni," Gichamba said furiously. "I want to know where Mugure and our car are. You have no business in any of this!"

"*Ati*, I want to know where Mugure and the car are," Wanjiru mimicked his accent, her lips twisted in a snarl. "Just what are they to you, eh? Was it *you* who won the car or Mugure?"

"It is my phone that drew the winning number, a phone which I bought with my own money," Gichamba retorted, stung. "The business is mine; it is *I* who opened it for my wife."

"What kind of a phone is that, eh?" Wanjiru said, mockingly. "Do you even know what phones look like?" Muthoni and Wanjiru exchanged amused glances, breaking into contemptuous laughter. "Come on, Muthoni, show him what a phone looks like."

"Listen, Gichamba," Muthoni said stepping forward, thrusting a finger in his face, "if it is a phone you want we can buy you a dozen phones. That thing you call a phone is nothing to us, do you hear? Come on, look at me!" She swiveled around like a peacock, her ample hips straining against the cloth of her *khanga*. "Do you think I look like someone who would be caught with a thing like that in my handbag?" Wanjiru cackled with derisive laughter. "Listen to me well, *kijana*. The truth of the matter is that you were not even there when the entry for the competition was made. Whose picture was in the newspapers? Was it yours or Mugure's?"

"Yes, answer us that," Wanjiru urged, her expression that of a hunter taking aim along the shaft of a tightly drawn arrow. "Whose picture was it, Gichamba?"

"I demand to speak to my wife!" Gichamba shouted, unable to contain his fury any longer. "Bring Mugure out here and let her swear to the things you are saying!"

"Listen, Gichamba," Muthoni said condescendingly. "I know you feel that we have robbed you. I would feel the same if I was in your place, and I will not waste any more of your time. First let me put you in the picture, if only to save you the heartache. The truth is that the car has been sold and the money is safely in the custody of Mugure's family. We reached this decision together, as a family. I will not tell you how much it was sold for, but I just want you to know that it has, and so you should stop dreaming about it. I hope we now understand each other?"

Gichamba stared at her for a long while, swallowed the lump in his throat, and nodded slowly as if he were coming out of a trance.

"Good. Secondly, I think you heard what *Mzee* said? He has never seen a goat's tail delivered to his compound as Mugure's dowry, neither has he tasted your beer. And so technically, you and Mugure have just been girlfriend and boyfriend and not really husband and wife. I know you will argue," she held up a hand to stifle his protest, "but the truth is that if you speak to someone who understands these matters they will tell you that *Mzee* is within his right as far as tradition goes. That is just the way it is, Gichamba. Now, I know it was you who bought Mugure the phone, and that you rightfully deserve a share of the prize. But like we said before the prize is hers—just as the phone company stated—and it is entirely up to her to do with it as she pleases."

"So why isn't Mugure telling me this?" Gichamba stammered, his heart a leaden weight in his chest.

"Please, let me finish," said Muthoni, her hand outstretched. "As I said I am only trying to lay it out for you. Arguing about it won't help matters. Now," she said quickly, before he could interrupt again, "this is what we are going to do. We are reasonable people, you see, and we recognize the fact that you were living with Mugure at the time when good fortune visited her. Because of that we shall not cast you away empty-handed. We have deliberated on the matter and agreed to give you a portion of the money. You will also have your phone back so that you can continue running the business in the hope of striking another fortune. As regards your relationship with Mugure, I am afraid it will depend on whether you decide to formally go and ask for her hand. I believe that is a matter between the two of you. Nonetheless if you asked me I'd advise you give it a shot. *Mzee* is not unreasonable. If you move with speed he might just give you his blessings. That, Gichamba, is how the matter stands. And if you will excuse me I will fetch the package for you." Muthoni gestured to Wanjiru, who came forward with the black elections observer's bag.

"I believe this is all that we owe you," said Muthoni calmly, laying the bag on the stair. "And now, if you are reasonable, you will take your bag and go. I believe this matter is settled."

Gichamba remained rooted to the spot as the two women watched him stonily, arms folded across their ample bosoms. He tried to speak, but his tongue felt swollen in his mouth.

"I hope we don't have to bring in the police," Muthoni said finally, her tone resuming the earlier iciness. "There is a police patrol base just down the road, and if I must, I will call and tell them that you are trespassing. Have a good day, Gichamba." With that she drew closed the little steel gate that secured the veranda entrance, turned on her heel, and disappeared into the house.

"Listen, you two," Gichamba shouted hoarsely, finding his voice at last, "this matter is not over! I will be back!"

The massive front door slammed behind them and

Gichamba could hear the sound of the bolt sliding shut. Slowly Gichamba retrieved his bag, slinging it over his shoulder as he slipped out between the iron gates. He glanced back at the house, hoping to catch a glimpse of Mugure in one of the windows, but the lace curtains were drawn and still.

That evening Gichamba got truly drunk for the first time since the day he had received news of their prize-winning car. In company with Ndirangu, he visited one pub after another until they staggered home, singing raucously, the black elections observer's bag dragging along the ground behind them. The following morning, after Gichamba had sobered up, he opened the black bag to discover his phone, along with a manila envelope containing two hundred and fifty thousand shillings—his share.

When he visited Muthoni's house in Wangige the following week, driven by a desire to see Mugure, he found a To Let sign hanging on the locked gate. A uniformed guard, who was patrolling the premises, gruffly informed him that the last tenant had left no forwarding address.

The girl was weary and footsore, her foam bathroom slippers worn at the heel, the straps held in place by twisted wire. The baby slept in the dirty *shuka*[79] slung across her back, her tiny toes and wooly head emerging from the pool of shade thrown by her mother's shaggy nest of unkempt hair. Occasionally the baby whimpered softly and sucked noisily at her thumb. The mother's gaze focused intently on the dusty road ahead, swaying slightly to the motion of the cloth bundle

---

[79] plain cotton sheet

balanced on her head. The murram road danced softly in the midday sun, the shimmering mirages rising off the hot surface, blurring her vision. Fighting a rising dizziness, she continued resolutely forward.

A cattle truck had brought her from Isiolo the day before, depositing her at the Kiamaiko market. She had wandered a while among the Somali goat traders, trying to find the trader who had robbed and raped her. She had intended to plead with him to return her ID and bank card. He could keep the money. Toward midday, having had no luck in discovering her attacker, she decided to board a *matatu* to town. She had a few coins hidden away in the knot in her *shuka*, enough to pay for the fare to town and a meal of *githeri*. The other passengers in the *matatu* had wrinkled their noses and turned their heads away when she had squeezed among them. She was, she knew, filthy and unkempt. Strands of straw and knotted burrs tangled in her hair, and raw scratch marks surrounded wounds where ticks had once attached themselves. If that were not enough, she smelled strongly of goats with which she had ridden in the back of the truck.

Her child had been born outside Isiolo town on the coarse grass behind a fawn-colored thorny bush. She could close her eyes and recall those hours with a vivid clarity—the coarse grass on which she lay, prickling the back of her bare thighs; between her trembling legs, across the mound of her belly, she could see the rickety *manyatta*[80] she had been attempting to reach before she collapsed. A shaggy-winged scavenging

---

[80] A traditional Maasai hut made by bending interlocking tree saplings, that are planted in the ground, into a dome shape and plastering the structure over with mud and cow dung.

bird, etched against the azure blue sky, sailed lazily on the thermal above as her breath labored in her throat, her spine stiffening in agony as the spasms of birth convulsed from one end of her body to the other. Through the deafening din in her ears she heard the sound of cowbells and voices.

Opening her eyes, she saw Maasai herdsmen crowded around her, leaning on their long white herding sticks and talking animatedly in a language she could not understand. She recognized, however, the glances of kind concern that flittered across their brown and weathered faces.

Later, as she nursed her baby in the shade of a thorn tree, she wished she might reward these kind herdsmen—who had not asked for a penny in payment. And yet they had quietly passed on, true to their ancient nomadic instinct to find the next green grazing patch for their herds.

Stumbling on a stone, she stubbed her toe on the murram road and stooped to rub her foot, a grimace curling her cracked lips. Then, straightening painfully, she limped around a bend in the road to see the *mabati*-roofed store the farm women had told her of. The road in front of the store was crowded with several trucks, half a dozen handcarts, and half a dozen people coming and going. The sign above the store read: Gichamba's Hardware Store, Dealers in Construction Material, Sand, and Ballast.

The girl stopped dead in her tracks, her eyes glued to the people at the counter, her heart drumming inside her chest. A boy perched high on a donkey cart paused to stare at her, the empty water barrel the beast was lugging to the stream stirring up dust behind them. The girl took no notice, but stared fixedly at the buxom woman behind the counter, who also carried a baby on her back. The woman moved with ease, despite her immense girth, chatting up the customers as she fetched their orders and wrote out their receipts. Behind her Gichamba struggled with a bundle of half-inch PVC pipes, trying to pull them out of the top rack without dislodging the rest. A battered Chevrolet pick-up truck backed up to the entrance, a cloud of black diesel smoke billowing past the counter and causing the woman to shout a blustery protest. The girl could see though that even as she yelled at the truck driver, wagging her finger in his direction, her chubby face was laughing, and her eyes friendly.

The driver climbed out and crushed a cigarette butt under the heel of his pointed boot. Then, thumbs hooked in the loops of his faded jeans, he sauntered up to the counter, pausing to tease the woman who waited behind it, slapping her upper arm playfully. After which, lifting the panel at the end of the counter, the driver assisted Gichamba with the pipes, carrying them in stacks out to the pick-up truck. The woman, perched on her high stool behind the counter, tallied each order in her receipt book as the men passed, her forefinger moving down the listed entries on the LPO form at her elbow.

After the pipes had been counted, packed, and secured, Gichamba paused, wiping the sweat from his brow. He turned and his eyes met those of the girl just as she was preparing to turn on her heel and bolt. Instinctively, he started forward, his eyes widening in sudden recognition. Clutching at the cloth bundle on her head, the other hand supporting the baby on her back, the girl turned and ran.

A battered Bedford truck hurtled up the road, lugging a

huge exhauster tank behind, delicately balanced on a rickety frame. The driver, seeing the girl run into the road, slammed on the brakes, cursing loudly, the smell of burnt rubber filling the air. The girl thudded against the steaming radiator grill and tumbled to the road, the bundle on her head rolling away into the gutter.

Gichamba reached her just as the driver and his loader leapt out of the cab, one to see to the girl and the other to wedge a rock under the wheel to prevent the truck from rolling downhill. Gichamba held the girl by one hand and the driver by the other as they helped her to her feet.

"Are you hurt?" the driver asked, dusting her off. "Is the baby all right?"

"Mugure!" Gichamba cried, clasping her by the shoulders and peering into her dusty face. "Is that really you?"

They stood by the road long after the exhauster truck had departed.

"You mean I have been a father all this while and yet I didn't know it?" he asked at length, gazing down into the bright dark eyes of the little one who nestled in his arms. Mugure nodded, not trusting her voice to reply.

"But…I mean, how…?"

"It is a long story," said Mugure faintly, adjusting the fold of the dusty *shuka* to shield the child from the overhead sun. "It needs time for the telling of it."

"*Ngai!* I can't believe this," Gichamba exclaimed, unable to take his eyes off the child. "Why didn't you ever tell me?"

"As I said it is a long story, Gichamba," Mugure said wearily, "and I am tired."

"Yes, I'm sorry." Gichamba raised his eyes to look at her. "Please forgive me. It has all been a shock to me. Come. You must be hungry. Let's go home," he said, reaching for her bundle.

"Wait," Mugure hesitated. "Is that your shop? I mean, is that where we are going?"

"Yes," said Gichamba. "I started it with the money Muthoni gave me."

"But…" Mugure began, glancing over at the woman who stood behind the shop counter, herself staring curiously at the two who stood by the dusty road.

"Oh, you wanted to ask about the woman?" Gichamba said with a smile. "That is my sister-in-law Njeri. Her husband is the driver of the Chevrolet truck. They are helping me run the business," he explained. "Is that why you were running away?"

Mugure lowered her gaze to her dusty feet.

"Come now, let's go and meet them. Njeri is a nice woman and the pillar of the business. She handles all the paperwork and can whittle a sale out of a miser. We landed several lucrative orders this past month that we are struggling to deliver on time, which is why we are so busy. Her husband Irungu oversees sand and ballast, while I handle the rest of the hardware deliveries. Ndirangu—do you remember him from my quarry days?—he handles the bigger truckloads when we need them. Come, Mugure," he said, tugging gently at her elbow. "Everyone on the street is staring at us."

She followed reluctantly.

That evening Gichamba sat with his family around the charcoal brazier in the little room at the back of the store. The shop had closed for the day and the Samburu guard they employed had taken up station by the front door to guard both the hired truck and the two handcarts. Gichamba rocked his sleeping daughter in his lap as he listened to Mugure recount the events that followed the sale of the Mercedes. He felt a heaviness in his heart as the extent of the treachery of her two handlers became apparent.

"They are a bunch of vipers," he cried, fighting back tears. "Your Aunt Muthoni and her friend are vicious gold-diggers!"

"You are right," Mugure admitted, recalling how her family had melted away when they sensed the money was running out. "I really had no right coming back into your life after everything I allowed them to do."

"Please don't say that, darling," Gichamba said, drawing her into an embrace. "Your aunt deceived us all. You don't know the agony I went through after they took you away. The store kept me sane. If it had not been for the work, I would have gone mad."

"It took winning the Mercedes for me to realize how few true friends we have in life," Mugure managed between sobs, "especially where money is concerned. I hope you can forgive me some day, Gichamba."

"I already have," Gichamba said gently, drying her tears with the baby's shawl.

"Thank you. Still…"

"Still what, my love?" said Gichamba, rubbing her shoulder.

"I don't know if I will fit in here," Mugure said, drying her eyes. "If your family will accept me after everything..."

"They already have, Mugure. We are back together, and this time no one will separate us. Now, let us put all that behind us and go to bed. We should be grateful we have each other. Truly we should. Come now; let us go to bed, my love."

And for the first time since the car came into their lives the young couple slept deeply, dreaming in each other's arms, the infant snuggled between them. It would take Njeri and her husband together banging on the front door to wake them late the following morning, well past the store's typical opening time. Customers were already lining up.

"Take the advice of an old hand, Gichamba. This woman is going to cost you your business," said Irungu jocularly when Gichamba finally opened the door. "I am an old hand at these matters you know," he added with a wink. To which the three of them laughed merrily.

"See? Gichamba finally has a smile back on his face," Njeri said, after the laughter had died down. "After only one night. And you men say you can live without women!"

Later in the day when business slackened Gichamba took his wife to the nearby police station so that they could fill out a form and start the lengthy process of acquiring a new ID for her. Thereafter they could access the one hundred and fifty thousand shillings that remained of the Mercedes proceeds, which were presently stuck in the bank.

ACKNOWLEDGEMENTS

I'd like to acknowledge the input of the late Susan Linnée, who was my first reader, critic, and editor, together with the late Patrick Adika, who always came in handy whenever Susan's old HP or my equally old Toshiba broke down, either due to a virus attack, a hardware malfunction, or a requisite software upgrade—there's no writer I know of who trusts their raw data in the hands of a stranger.

Also Michela Wrong, who believed in what I was doing, and walked the talk—the reason the journey came a cropper is known to you and I; Khainga "le President" Okwemba of PEN Kenya; Barbara Njau and Kudakwashe Kamupira of Bahati Books, London; Prof Shaul Bassi, Chiara Lunardelli, Stefano Chinellato and the entire team I worked with at Università Ca' Foscari, Venezia.

Lastly is Jaynie Royal and her entire team at Regal House Publishing, who eventually delivered the baby.

Thank you so much.

Gazemba S. A, Nairobi, 2018.